PRAISE BE TO SILVER

Framed for the killing of an assay agent in the Colorado town of Green Ridge, Morgan Silver escapes the lethal attentions of a vigilante mob by the skin of his teeth. With his new identity he heads south, but fate in the shape of the real killer appears, and thwarts his every move. Fortunately, Lady Luck steps in once again to aid the fugitive — but he will need nerves of steel and a steady hand to clear his name . . .

Books by Ethan Flagg
in the Linford Western Library:

TWO FOR TEXAS
DIVIDED LOYALTIES
DYNAMITE DAZE
APACHE RIFLES
DUEL AT DEL NORTE
OUTLAW QUEEN
WHEN LIGHTNING STRIKES

ETHAN FLAGG

PRAISE BE TO SILVER

Complete and Unabridged

LINFORD
Leicester

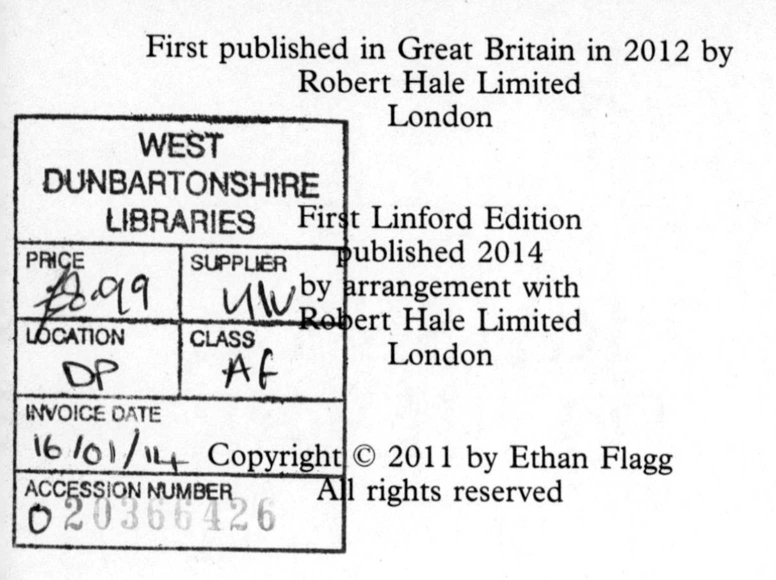

First published in Great Britain in 2012 by
Robert Hale Limited
London

First Linford Edition
published 2014
by arrangement with
Robert Hale Limited
London

*A catalogue record for this book is available
from the British Library.*

ISBN 978–1–4448–1850–5

Published by
F. A. Thorpe (Publishing)
Anstey, Leicestershire

Set by Words & Graphics Ltd.
Anstey, Leicestershire
Printed and bound in Great Britain by
T. J. International Ltd., Padstow, Cornwall

This book is printed on acid-free paper

1

Cast Afoot

The tall rider drew his mount to a halt.

Exhibiting a casual sense of well-being, he surveyed the lonely terrain. Serried ranks of dark green pine rose up on either side. Freeman Pass was the only rent cutting through the impregnable bulwark of Colorado's Grape Mountains.

The narrow gap was named after the intrepid explorer who helped map the territory and make it safe for future immigrants using the famed Oregon Trail. Gold prospectors later passed this way in their search for paydirt.

Morgan Silver had been one of them. But that was before he discovered that making a quick buck from mining was more a case of luck than good judgement for a tenderfoot miner. A lazy smile passed over the handsome visage as his narrowing gaze scanned the lie of the land ahead.

Below, down a tortuous trail lay the plateaulands of the Chavez Saltflats. It was a blanched waterless landscape from which there was no escape; that is unless a traveller felt it more prudent to take the wide detour by way of Salida to the west. But that would entail a further seven days' ride.

Morgan was not prepared to accept such a delay.

He had already been on the trail for two weeks and was anxious to reach his destination. The last two nights had been spent resting up in Cripple Creek. That had been his first real opportunity to celebrate the good fortune that had come his way since leaving the northern Colorado boom town of Idaho Springs. A few drinks and some proper food were a welcome respite from the open-air night camps.

With this in mind, he was more than willing to splash out on the luxury of a large feather bed with clean sheets.

But now it was time to be moving on. Not the most patient of men, Morgan could barely contain his excitement. For the fifth time that day, he pulled the officially stamped and sealed document from inside his jacket and avidly perused the contents.

Another loose smile cracked the rider's taciturn demeanour. Slowly it spread across the chiselled profile burgeoning into a contented grin. Yes indeed, life was sure looking rosy for the retired gold prospector. Here in his hand was the chance to fulfil his dream of becoming a rancher with a spread of his own in the Texas panhandle.

This Shangri-La was a further week's ride to the south east.

Six years of grinding toil in the goldfields of Tumbleweed to the north west of Denver had produced little in the way of a decent grubstake for the Missouri immigrant. It was not until he lit upon a far more lucrative, and infinitely more congenial business opportunity in the mining camp of Idaho Springs that enough funds could be salted away to furnish his dream.

Originally called Jackson's Diggings after the prospector who first discovered the gold seam, the boom town became Idaho Springs when the medicinal healing properties of the hot springs became apparent in 1874.

Health seekers came from Denver and beyond to take advantage of the soothing balm. Such was the influx that an enterprising individual able to harness nature's elixir and sell it in bottled form would be sure to make his poke in no time.

Morgan Silver was just such a man.

The paydirt he had saved was enough to finance the venture.

Within weeks he had organized the logistics of the operation under the slogan of *Doctor Elias Crimble's Patent Balm — A soothing restorative for all manner of muscular ailments*. Sales to distant townships as far afield as Chicago and St Louis were quickly established.

Although initially successful, Morgan Silver was no hard-headed business tycoon. His was a crude operation lacking the finesse of more astute promoters. These rivals were quickly able to bring a more professional backing to their enterprises, which began to undercut Morgan's profits.

After six months the writing was on the wall. Sell out or go under.

He sold to the highest bidder and immediately tendered for a piece of prime cattle country advertised in the *Denver Post*. The bid was successful and the contract signed.

And Morgan was now on his way to take possession of his dream. Slipping the heavy parchment back into his pocket, his left hand tapped the thick leather of his saddle-bag which contained the deposit of two thousand dollars.

Morgan conceded that he had been lucky. And a man has to take full advantage of the cards dealt to him in this life.

Hooded brown eyes filtered out the hot noonday sun as he scanned the bleak terrain of the saltflats. He nudged the horse forward, slowly descending the stony trail as it picked a zig-zagged course down from the pass. The desolate nature of the arid landcape held no fears for the mossyhorn rancher.

Again he patted the bags crammed full of greenbacks. Nothing was going to stop Morgan Silver from realizing a life-long ambition. A dreamy cast smoothed out the rugged contours of his face, his mind drifting towards a secure future. Stroking his luxurious black moustache, thoughts of a new name for the ranch jostled for position inside his head.

Satisfied musings drifted off at a tangent as he considered the possibilities. Circle S, Barred MS, M Diamond S? There again, the Steaming Springs Ranch sounded good.

So intent was Morgan on conjuring up all the things he would do upon reaching the Brazos country that he completely failed to heed the sinister fact that danger was rapidly crowding in on the lone rider.

The first he realized that all was not as it should be was the constricting bite of twin lariats tightening about his chest. Before he could react, Morgan was jerked roughly from the saddle. He landed with a heavy thud.

This sudden change in fortune knocked the breath from his body.

A harshly grating laugh penetrated the dense fug of his stupified brain.

'This is gonna be a sight easier than we figured, boys.'

The gruff speaker was accompanied by three other hard-faced jaspers who aimed mirthless grins down at their squirming captive.

'Get the bastard on his feet!' the leader of the disparate bunch of roughnecks snapped out brusquely.

Rufus Cahill was a heavy-set critter

in his early forties. He was clad in worn range garb, the distinctive red vest now white with dried salt. A grizzled beard concealed much of his gnarled features. But there was no mistaking the avaricious glint that sparkled in the wide-set black eyes.

Nor the well-oiled Smith & Wesson double action Schofield revolver clutched in his meaty fist.

A half-breed Commanche buck who answered to the name of Black Dog Boone immediately leaped off his roan and began tugging the boots from the victim's feet. At the same time, he grabbed the guy's Stetson, stuck an eagle feather in the hat band and proudly slammed it on to his own head. The breed's beady eyes were already stripping Silver of his other clothes.

Where his paleface compadres valued that which could buy them a good time, the Indian was more concerned with being treated as an equal. In order to be fully accepted by the other members of the band, Black Dog figured he had to look like them.

And this guy's duds were store-bought, unlike his own tribal-made buckskins. Harder wearing perhaps, but that was irrelevant. They lacked the kudos of the white man's apparel.

'Leave that 'til later,' rasped Cahill acidly. 'Check his saddle-bags for the dough.'

Boone's mouth twisted but he reluctantly obeyed, joining a stocky Mexican called Gonzales. They quickly confirmed the boss's supposition that their quarry was toting a hefty wad of cash.

A wide toothy grin split the Mexican's swarthy face as he lifted out a thick bunch of greenbacks.

'Is here, boss,' Gonzales called out, waving the notes in the hot air. 'You were right. There is enough to buy favours of the finest *señoritas* in Salida.' His leering visage adopted a dreamy cast at the thought.

Morgan attempted to shake the

numbing effects of the ambush from his brain. It was an uphill struggle that failed miserably as he tried freeing himself from the tight confines of the lariats.

A savage blow to the head from the pistol butt of a fourth member of the gang sent him tumbling back into the dust. Cactus Jack Selman uttered a throaty laugh. The chilling sound emerged as a choking cough. The gunman relished the power such actions bestowed almost as much as the rewards of operating outside the law.

Groans of pain from the victim went unheeded.

'Pass those bags over here,' ordered Cahill who was casually eyeballing the proceedings from atop his large bay. Gonzales handed the heavy bag up to the boss who quickly rifled through them. He gave a curt nod of satisfaction. 'More here than I figured,' he enthused, smiling. 'We can add some bottles of five star French brandy to them saloon gals you mentioned, Gonzales.'

'*Sí, sí, patrón*, it is as you say,' chirped up the Mexican. In his excitement, the lyrical cadence was enhanced to a sing-song warble. 'And this must be the best payday for us this year.'

'You ain't wrong there,' agreed Cahill. His next comment was directed at the Indian. 'OK, Boone,' he sneered, injecting the instruction with a disparaging tone that was lost on the Indian but received knowing leers from the others, 'strip this critter down to his underwear if'n you've a mind.'

Black Dog needed no second bidding.

Within two minutes Morgan Silver was left sprawled in the dust clad only in a set of dirty pink johns that had seen better days. Even Boone had balked at removing them.

The Indian had taken everything else, even down to the socks that left a nose-twitching odour in their wake.

Soon he was proudly strutting around the site of the recent ambush eliciting the air of a haughty peacock.

The others laughed at him. But their disdainful cracks went over the breed's head. A spirited display of the latest nickel-plated Remington .44 revolver was enough to staunch any further scorn.

'OK, you guys! Enough of this catterwallin',' rasped the gang leader impatiently as he swung his horse round. 'Get this fella secured to that cotton-wood, then we'll split the breeze pronto.'

The victim was hustled over to the tree and roughly pinioned to the trunk. Head drooping over his chest, and barely conscious of his surroundings, a thin trail of blood trickled down his neck. So abrupt had been the attack that Silver had been unable to respond.

Raucous bellows from the bushwackers heehawing their derision barely registered in the stricken man's brain. His head felt like a blacksmith was hammering to get out.

'Should I drill him, boss?' hollered a leering Selman. Brandishing a large .36 Remington-Ryder, he was just itching to haul back on the trigger. The hammer snapped back in fevered anticipation.

Cahill leaned over the neck of his cayuse and peered down at the brutalized recipient of his ambush from beneath thick black brows. He stroked the greasy beard while giving the suggestion serious consideration. An ugly grin eventually revealed yellowed teeth.

'Sure thing, Cactus, why not?' The query was not intended to be questioned. 'It'll give us some target practice.'

The others laughed uproariously at this quip. All except Gonzales who now stepped forward.

'Why not allow this fellow to suffer by leaving him tied to tree,' he argued prodding the drooping torso of the tethered captive. 'No water in this heat?

He might last one day, two maybe. Give him chance to think on what he has lost.' Now Gonzales evinced a hearty chortle. 'And perhaps give thanks that his generosity has helped to improve the lot of us poor travellers.'

Cahill was taken aback by the Mexican's rhetoric. His hard face assumed a frosty mien. Then he released a rasping guffaw of his own.

'You're right, Gonzales,' he pronounced. 'Maybe the poor dupe has suffered enough for one day.' The conclusive verdict, thick with sardonic humour, was not meant to be challenged.

Selman grunted. The hardcase's lip twisted but he said nothing.

'It's your lucky day, fella,' Cahill continued breezily. 'That heap of dough has put ole Rufus in a right dandy mood.' Again he studied the pinioned captive before adding with nonchalent disdain, 'Then again, in your present situation, maybe you ain't so lucky after all.'

And with that mercurial comment fizzing on the soft breeze, he galloped off followed by his hallooing bunch of ne'er-do-well brigands.

Within minutes silence had once again enfolded the grim terrain.

But it was a further half hour before Morgan was able to shake off the bruising effects of the ambush. His head still felt like it had been kicked by a mule, but at least he could now think straight. And the clarity of awareness did not make for a positive evaluation of his predicament.

All but naked, unarmed and cast afoot, not to mention the theft of his land deposit. Worst of all he had been left bound tighter than a Thanksgiving turkey. Unless he could get free, the grim reaper would surely come a-calling. And soon.

Raging wildly, he cursed the parentage of the ambushers. The maniacal raving made the captive feel no better. Indeed, the fervent attempts to break free only served to tighten the bonds even further. Silver quickly realized that such futile endeavours were as likely to succeed as a guardian angel suddenly appearing with a knife.

A black depression settled over the stricken captive.

It was five minutes later that a faint twittering penetrated his morbid ruminations. Wearily raising his head, Morgan noticed a tiny lark perched on the grubby buckskin breechclout discarded by Black Dog. More interesting, however, was the elkhorn grip of what had to be a knife poking from beneath the garment. The breed must have been so intent on admiring his new duds that such incidentals had passed unnoticed.

Morgan's whole body tensed. Was it close enough to win?

Stretching out his foot, he strained with all his might to reach the ellusive means of escape.

Two inches short! So near yet so far.

He cried out in frustration.

Then a miracle happened. One of those freakish chances in a million that come along at just the right moment.

A rattlesnake shot from beneath the clout. But it was not the helpless human that was in the hungry reptile's sights. The snake struck with deadly intent, its death-dealing pair of poison-packers latching on to the unfortunate winged wanderer. With barely a pause for breath, the attacker quickly slithered away to devour its prey at leisure elsewhere.

The creature's sudden lunge had judiciously caught the knife, tilting it towards the captive. This time, Morgan's wriggling toes were able to drag the all-important blade closer. By swivelling his body around the narrow trunk of the cottonwood, he could then reach it from behind with his fingers.

Sawing through the tough hemp ropes that secured him was a slow and awkward task. His fingers bled, the knife frequently slipping. But this was his only chance to get free.

An hour later, his exhausted frame fell away from the trunk. Splayed out on the ground, he lay still, unable even to summon up the strength to raise himself off the ground. Breathing deeply, he offered up thanks to his Maker, the feathered angel that had given its life, and even the deadly rattler for delivering him from a hideous demise.

Or had they?

Having been released from one torment, another had now been placed in his path: how to reach civilization? Lacking any form of bodily sustenance, walking out of there barefoot was certain to be a tall order.

Was it asking too much, a task too far? Indeed, had Morgan Silver jumped from the proverbial frying pan into the fire?

There was only one way to find out.

2

Praise Be!

Alice Bishop yipped at the half dozen calves jogging along the trail ahead of her. She was one of that new breed of frontier women who liked to think she was doing her bit for the cause of feminist equality. And that certainly did not include merely serving the menfolk with their bodily sustenance.

Her pa was constantly exorting her to wear dresses and act the part of the dutiful daughter. But Alice had other ideas.

'You're never gonna find yourself a good husband wearin' jeans and check shirts all the time,' he endlessly carped.

Thus far Alice had resisted his remonstrations knowing she had the ageing cowman wrapped around her little finger. Not that Alice was a poor cook. Her apple dumplings and beef stew had won prizes at the local county shows.

But where other young ladies settled into the mundane chores of home-building, Alice regarded herself as a free spirit. Flower arranging and dress-making were not for her. She enjoyed nothing better than riding the range and helping out with the huge array of tasks required to run a successful ranch like the Praise B.

And that included rounding up stray mavericks.

Alice Bishop was most definitely a comely young colt; one who might conservatively be termed easy on the eye. The range gear she opted to sport only served to enhance her allure. And the hands were more than eager to teach the girl everything there was to learn.

Although it was towards her slim and shapely contours that their eyes were invariably drawn.

Alice, however, was totally immune to

the rivalry for her attention among the Praise B cowpokes. The macho posturing that accompanied the instruction likewise went completely over her head.

Only on a Sunday did the girl deign to regail herself in female accoutrements when she accompanied her father to church.

Clayton Bishop had assumed the role of preacher in the local township of Salida in the absence of a full-time incumbent of the office. And he took his duties seriously. Being a rancher during the week, Clay was able to reach out to the spiritual needs of a community where the longhorn was king. Due to recent commitments on the ranch, however, he had had to forego his spiritual duties for the last month.

Branding had to come first at this time of year.

The girl smiled to herself. She loved her father deeply. But he was stuck in a time warp. Women growing up in the 1870s were rapidly emerging from their shell. They wanted a more prominent say in the country's future. And Alice wanted to be at the front of the parade.

Such futuristic notions were clamouring for attention inside her head as she cantered along the trail. The red hair beneath the flat plainsman was caught by the gentle zephyrs. Streaming out behind her it allowed the sunlight to catch the fiery tresses giving her the mystical appearance of a winged messenger of the gods.

Narrowed eyes scanned the rough clumps of sagebrush and thorn on either side of the trail searching out other calves that had escaped the recent branding session.

But it was a flurry of circling buzzards away over to her right that suddenly caught the girl's attention. She frowned. Her freckled nose twitched. Something wasn't right. Maybe it was an injured calf and those critters were just waiting for it to die before picking the bones clean.

'What d'yuh say, Beauty?' she murmured to the grey Appaloosa. 'Reckon we oughta take a peek over there?'

The horse snickered, its patrician head bobbing in agreement.

'You shouldn't oughta be wandering off alone, Miss Alice,' observed her companion, a tall negro whose bald pate reflected the sunlight in the manner of a looking glass.

The girl sighed.

'You watch these critters, Sam,' she said arrowing a meaningful look at the fretting cowhand. 'I won't tell Pa if'n you don't. 'Sides, I'll only be a couple of ticks.'

Without waiting for a response, she nudged the grey off the trail. Cocked-eyed Sam arranged his oddball scrutiny into some sort of order. An overblown shrug of apparent indifference pursued the girl as she galloped away. In truth, Sam was devoted to Alice. He had been allotted the task of looking after her when she insisted on heading off into the brush. It was the one concession she had been forced to accept in order to win her father over.

Sam, nobody knew his full name, was likewise zealously attached to the ranch owner. Clay Bishop had rescued him from a severe beating when the black man had inadvertently strayed into an all-white bar in Amarillo.

The strange glassy appearance that had resulted in his nickname hadn't helped matters. Sam could have easily managed a couple of adversaries. But Clay regarded seven-to-one odds as being chicken-livered. He watched for a spell before stepping in with the butt end of a shotgun.

The unequal contest was quickly terminated.

Clay soon found that his Good Samaritan endeavour had produced a life-long admirer. The guy took to following him around like a faithful hound. Unable to shake him off, Clay did the next best thing and offered him a job.

So here he was. Cock-eyed Sam, ex-slave

and cottonpicker, now employed for dollar wages on the Praise B cattle ranch. Black as the ace of spades, he couldn't have been more proud.

Watching the girl disappear into the dusty wasteland, his ebony features tensed up with some trepidation.

The lascivious attention of the hovering predators was towards the far side of some rocks crowning a low knoll. Mounting the hillock, Alice's eagle eye latched on to a bundle of dirty pink rags slumped over a boulder. Moving closer she soon picked out a bare foot poking out, then an arm.

Her green eyes bulged wide. An involuntary scream of fear escaped from her open mouth as she realized it was a human being.

Cock-eyed Sam heard the fretful cry and immediately dug his spurs into the flanks of the tough little mustang. On reaching the far side of the hill, he saw his charge bending over a hump. Gun in hand, he galloped up and leapt out of the saddle.

'Y-you OK, missy?' he stammered, pointing the old .31 Whitney at the supine form lying still on the ground. 'Is that fella still alive?'

'Sure is, Sam. But only just. The poor guy's unconscious and in bad shape.' She hauled the dead weight on to some level ground. Then, addressing her worried chaperone, she rapped, 'Pass me your water bottle. His face and mouth are blistered raw.'

Snatching hold of the proffered item, she dribbled the precious liquid over the ravaged contours of the man's lacerated face and lips. His feet were bleeding from numerous cuts.

Apart from suffering the brutal effects of over-exposure to the blazing sun, Morgan Silver didn't appear to be otherwise incapacitated. He was lucky. Another few hours and he would have surely been a goner.

Nonetheless, it was imperative they took him back to the ranch for some proper medication.

* * *

The patient's eyes opened slowly, tentatively, as if afraid that he might witness his own demise. Stiff and aching muscles, however, informed the injured man that somehow he must have escaped the grim reaper's perditious attentions. Silver groaned aloud.

The noise brought a shuffling response from the far side of the bed.

'Thank heavens you're back with us.' The fervent remark was punched out with vigour. 'Praise be to the Lord.' Alice Bishop held the large family Bible in a tight grip and raised her head towards the heavens.

She had been sitting with the injured man almost constantly during the five days he had lain unconscious. Sleeping on the spare cot, she had only left the room to answer calls of nature and prepare some medicinal concoctions that were carefully administered to the blistered torso.

'Pa! Pa!' she called out. 'He's woken up.'

Clay Bishop hustled into the room just as the injured man was trying to raise himself on to one elbow.

'W-where a-am I?' The first words uttered by the patient emerged as a slurred croak. Watery eyes peered around, blearily taking in the agreeable surroundings. 'What is this place?'

By rights Silver figured he ought to be in Hell. Yet instead he had somehow been transported to an idyllic utopia.

Blue sky was framed by the open window of the room beside which hung green velvet drapes. Flowered paper covered the walls and a lightly scented aroma assailed his nasal passageway. This was certainly no rough masculine domain into which he had mysteriously wandered, more like a lady's boudoir.

Alice eased him back on to the feather pillow.

'You're at the Praise B ranch, fella, in Colorado,' a low baritone voice gently informed him.

'Now take it easy,' admonished the dulcet tones of a female. The ministering angel then proceeded to wipe away the sweat from his feverish brow. 'You've been hurt bad. We found you out on the flats all burned up . . . '

But the patient had once again fallen into the arms of Orpheus. An irregular sough informed the hovering saviours that there was still a fair way to go before this enigmatic stranger would be fully recovered from his ordeal.

'You need some rest yourself, gal,' chided her father. 'Why not take a break and let Sam keep watch?'

'Not until he's out of danger.'

Alice was adamant. This was her responsibility. And she intended to see it through, to the bitter end if need be. The fact that she had taken to the handsome stranger remained hidden, locked away, her secret.

A further week went by before Morgan was on his feet.

The blisters caused by the fierce sun had scabbed over and no longer pained him. But he could scarcely recognize the image that stared back through the mirror hanging on his bedroom wall. And that wasn't only on account of somebody having removed all traces of facial hair. Blotchy, red welts covered the clean-shaven face.

Glancing down, he could see that his feet were little better. But at least now he could wear boots padded out with thick socks.

All the stiffness had gone. And apart from his ravaged face, which he knew would heal in time, all appeared well. And it was all thanks to the hospitality of the Praise B. Special gratitude was reserved for Alice Bishop to whom Morgan had grown quite attached during his convalescence.

* * *

Two weeks had passed since Morgan had been so fortuitously dragged back from the portals of the great beyond. He was only too well aware as to his fate had not the lovely Alice and her stoic guardian happened along when they did. And he had not been backward in making her aware of his eternal gratitude for saving his life.

The pair had become rather more than just nurse and patient.

But Morgan knew he had to rein in his feelings. There was still the small matter of two thousand dollars outstanding, as well as a burning itch deep within his craw to exact a terminal retribution for his suffering.

Such issues could not be ignored.

As far as Morgan Silver was concerned, there could be no future for the pair until this had been completed to his satisfaction.

And now that he felt fully recovered from his ordeal, he was anxious to hit the trail. The longer he let the situation lie dormant, the harder it would be to flush the varmints out.

Father and daughter were sitting across the large dining table from their house guest. When Morgan voiced his concerns, Clay Bishop was of the opinion that he should allow the law to handle the matter. Alice fluttered her long eyelashes hoping to dissuade their guest from placing himself in further danger. The girl's doleful expression induced a momentary pang of guilt in the young man's heart.

But no amount of persuasion to resist taking a vigilante stance would sway the plainspoken Missourian.

'I'm much obliged for your advice, Mr Bishop,' he replied, 'but I ain't got much hope of no tinstar running these critters to earth.'

Morgan balked at expounding on his derogatory cynicism. He had his own reasons for not revealing that he had little faith in the legal process. And these were best left unsaid. Luckily, Clay Bishop didn't pursue the matter.

Realizing that the young man's mind was made up, the rancher shrugged as he lowered his head back to his meal. A rather constrained atmosphere settled over the small gathering.

The Chinese cook, Lee Fong, was hovering nearby and all three diners were relieved when the little man interrupted the rather uneasy silence.

'You like cooking, Mr Morgan, sir?' trilled Fong, his long black plait waving about like a bull whip. 'Plenty more for hungry patient?'

Morgan wiped his mouth on a napkin.

'Sure beats trail grub any day,' he enthused with genuine relish. 'Ain't had vittles this good in a coon's age.'

The frisky cook leapt about in delight before refilling their coffee cups.

It gave Morgan the opportunity to reclaim lost ground. No way did he want to create any friction after receiving such fine hospitality from the rancher and his daughter.

'How's things at the Praise B?' he asked while sipping the potent Arbuckles. 'Hear tell the cattle business is on the up since the army built that new post at Fort Calhoolie.'

Bishop's craggy features clouded over.

'Sure oughta be,' he replied brusquely. But his tone was downcast.

Morgan caught on to the fact that things were not hunky-dory on the ranch.

'Some'n wrong, Mr Bishop?'

'We've been losing cattle.' The rancher's voice had dropped to a flat coldness. 'Over the last couple of weeks, steers have gone missing from the north range.'

'What does the law have to say about it?' Morgan tried to keep the disdain from his voice.

'Tubb Ricketts is the local sheriff,' replied Bishop fixing a baleful eye on to the dregs of his coffee cup. 'He's a new guy brought in to replace the previous lawman who had some kinda mysterious accident. Mighty strange I call it,' he muttered shaking his head. 'One day here, the next poking up the daisies in the cemetery. Mighty strange.

'Anyways. I ain't met the new fella. It

was my top hand, Will Tennant, who reported the theft. He said that the sheriff reckons it's probably drifters just passing through and more'n likely just a one off. He claims there should be no difficulty catching up with the rustlers before they reach the rail head at Canon City.'

Morgan remained silent. His features were set hard as concrete. He did not have Bishop's confidence.

The older man paused. His chiselled contours were still drawn and anxious, as if he had read Morgan's thoughts and was not convinced either.

'Some'n else wrong, Mr Bishop?'

Before responding, the rancher stood up and walked over to the front window of the ranch house. Shoulders stooped, his poignant gaze was fixed on to the distant horizon where bunched cumulus dusted the tops of the mountains.

'It didn't stop at that,' he said. 'Another twenty head went missing only a couple of days ago.' His right arm swept across the distant panorama.

'My land stretches to the foothills of the Grapes. The boys have been keeping their eyes open, but they've a heap of range to look after as well as their normal chores. This is a busy time of year with branding an' all.'

Morgan saw the hurt in the older man's sunken features as his daughter joined him. She placed a comforting arm around his shoulders while taking over the clarification of their concerns.

Morgan waited, his body tense with unease. He drew hard on a cigar allowing the blue smoke to drift from between clenched teeth.

'The Top Dog Trading Company in Salida has signed a contract with the army for beef,' Alice explained, 'which leaves us out in the cold. We can either sell at a knock-down price to that scheming rat T. D. Webb who runs the Top Dog, or drive them to the nearest railhead.'

'And that's the Rio Grande Western at Canon City which is a four week drive,' interjected the irascible rancher.

Unable to contain his wrath, Clay Bishop slammed an angry fist against the wall. A hanging picture rattled in its frame. The jumpy cook quickly departed to avoid attracting his irate employer's wrathful attention.

'Don't worry, Pa,' Alice soothed trying to relieve the old man's distress. She knew exactly how to calm his sudden displays of temper. 'We'll figure some way to beat these varmints.'

The rancher managed to simmer down under the girl's gentle ministrations but gave his daughter a look of woeful cynicism.

'Maybe Ricketts will be able to run 'em down,' he voiced. 'Let's hope so.' But there was no conviction in the assertion.

Morgan was equally sceptical. Clearly a pragmatic approach was required.

With this in mind the Missourian's thoughts had been racing faster than a thoroughbred stallion. His brow furrowed. Perhaps he could help the rancher to recover the stolen cattle. If he could pull it off, at least that would be one dilemma solved. And wasn't he beholden to them for saving his bacon?

A steely resolve settled over the craggy features.

'First thing in the morning,' he averred firmly having reached a decision, 'I'm heading out in search of these rustlers. It's one way to pay my dues after all you've done for me.'

'This ain't your problem,' protested Bishop although a gleam of hope now flickered in the old guy's rheumy eyes.

'Well I'm making it mine.'

The declaration was delivered with solid conviction and brooked no rebuttal. Morgan held the older man's stark regard but it was the rancher who was first to lower his gaze.

'OK, Morgan. Have it your way,' he said. 'But I insist that you take Cock-eyed Sam with you. Agreed?'

'Don't forget me.' Both men stared open-mouthed at the girl. They were about to protest when she held up her hand. 'There's no use trying to dissuade me. I'm going and that's that.' Without uttering another word, she stamped out of the dining room, head held aloft.

'Ain't nothing you can do when she sets her mind,' sighed Bishop, arms raised in surrender. 'Just like her mother. Feisty as a wild mustang and twice as ornery.'

3

Rustlers' Roost

Early the next morning the three riders headed off in the direction of the north range. That was where the cattle had gone missing and it seemed like the best place to start. Initially composed of rolling grassland, the terrain became much rougher as they neared the foothills of the Grape Mountains.

The hazy outline of serrated peaks slowly sharpened into a more distinct configuration. Morgan was soon able to understand why the rustlers had selected such a place from which to conduct their nefarious enterprise.

Innumerable dried up arroyos and draws branched off in all directions. Searching through them would require a small army. Morgan's gaze hardened. The rustling of the Praise B cattle was clearly not the work of idle drifters. And another notion occurred to his agile brain. Choosing this time of year before most of the cattle had been branded with their mark of ownership had not been an accident.

This was the work of a determined gang. Skunks who were prepared to defend their haul with loaded guns.

For the time being, Morgan decided to keep his suspicions quiet. No sense in causing Alice any unnecessary anxiety until he was certain that his inklings were well founded.

They moved slowly around a large herd that was grazing a half mile from where the rising ground commenced. The closer they got to the foothills, the sparser the grass cover became. Quite suddenly, mesquite and cholla cactus took over as the dominant vegetation.

A fairly distinct line could be seen where the hoof-prints of the cattle ended. Even dumb beasts know where the best feed has terminated.

Riding along the edge of the plainly

visible tracks, Morgan urged his two confederates to keep their eyes peeled.

'Watch out for any sign that points to steers having been driven off the range. That way we can see which direction the rustlers have taken.'

For upwards of an hour narrowed eyes avidly scanned the terrain searching for the all-important indicators. But they found nothing.

Morgan was becoming frustrated; his mouth set in a hard line. Cattle had been rustled which meant there had to be tracks leading away from the main herd. But where were they? Had the rustlers taken a different route?

All his instincts screamed out that lawbreakers would want to conceal their thieving actions. And that meant using the harsh landscape to full effect. His gaze strayed towards the entrances to the numerous draws.

Steers can't fly. So where were they?

He scratched his head. Somewhere in that labyrinth was a ruthless bunch of cattle thieves who were probably at this very moment planting their own brand on the rumps of Praise B steers.

It was Cock-eyed Sam who offered a solution to their predicament.

'These rustlers are crafty fellas,' warbled the ex-slave. 'My guess is they rubbed out trail until inside one of the draws.'

Morgan's face lit up.

'You ain't just a perty face, Sam,' he called, a fresh wave of expectation tingling down his spine. 'Now why in tarnation didn't I think of that?'

'Perhaps because you not yet cattleman, sir,' replied the big negro respectfully. Having been a part of Morgan's rescue, Sam had been made privy to the Missourian's efforts to secure a foothold in the ranching business. 'I came across this trick while riding for an Arkansas outfit back in '69.' Sam then panned a raised arm over the line of broken foothills. 'If we ride along the edge of the rough country, we's sure to come across tracks sometime.'

'Then what are we waiting for?' Morgan swung his mount towards the foothills. 'How about you starting on the western side, with me and Alice coming from the east?' he suggested realizing that he was indeed a tenderfoot in this game. 'Then we can meet in the middle.'

'Good idea,' agreed Sam.

It was becoming patently clear that this aspect of the cattle business was deadly serious. There was a more than even chance that blood would be spilled. And the solid presence of the resolute and loyal negro was more than a touch welcome.

Morgan threw a concerned glance towards his willowy companion. But Alice appeared to have read his thoughts.

'Don't worry none about me,' she averred with spirited vigour tapping the rosewood stock of the Winchester rifle poking from its saddle boot. 'This long gun ain't just for show. That right, Sam?'

'Sure is,' concurred her faithful minder, 'Miss Alice can bring down a charging jack rabbit at two hundred paces.'

The girl's peppery rejoinder had taken Morgan aback. Never previously had he encountered such a self-assured female. It was both exhilarating and unsettling at the same time. He turned away to conceal the puzzled frown cloaking his features.

It was all right shooting at critters, but how would she behave when faced with a hard-bitten gunman whose sole intention was to drill her full of lead?

Slapping his mount on the rump, Morgan thundered away towards the line of bluffs rising up from the plains. Alice followed, easily keeping pace.

It was an hour later. Eyes peeled, they had come across nary a sign of cattle movement along any of the draws and arroyos. Morgan was beginning to feel that Cock-eyed Sam's theory was all hogwash when a piercing holler from Alice drew his immediate attention.

'Over there!' she yelled excitedly. A flurry of yellow dust rose above the broken line of sandstone bluffs.

A minute later, Sam came galloping round a bend. Dodging between the stands of spiny cactus and sagebrush, he skidded to a halt. His left arm pointed back the way he had come.

'Them bad guys used a draw some two miles back aways,' he panted unhooking the water bottle from his saddle-horn and taking a long swallow. 'Them sure is crafty dudes. I nearly missed it.' He paused for another swig of water. 'They've done a good job of hiding them tracks. Lucky for me they missed a couple near the entrance.'

The trio returned to the gap in the hills where Sam pointed out the all-important hoof prints.

Morgan dismounted to examine the indentations.

'These are steer marks all right,' he concurred. 'Well done, Sam.' The negro's shiny face split in a broad grin.

'And it looks like those are the hunks of mesquite they used to brush out the trail,' he added walking over to some discarded branches and examining the split ends. 'These are newly cut which means they can't be too far ahead of us.'

Remounting, Morgan nudged the saddle pony into the cleft where the prints of the rustled steers were clearly visible. The newcomer was learning fast.

From here on, all they had to do was follow the trail. But Morgan was well aware they would need to be in a state of constant alert. There was no telling how far ahead the rustlers were.

'Keep a watchful eye open,' he warned.

'Do you think they'll have a guard posted?' inquired Alice tentatively, a nervous inflection sullying her query now that the confrontation with the rustlers was drawing near.

'My guess is they'll figure to have outwitted any pursuers with their crafty manoeuvre using the sagebrush sweepers.' He rolled a stogie while aiming his next remark at Cock-eyed Sam. 'But thanks to this smart cookie, we've gotten the whip hand now.' His mouth tightened into a compressed line of determination. 'We have to make certain of keeping it.'

For the next three hours the grim threesome followed the trail left by the stolen cattle. Fidgety and becoming more skittish as time wore on, anxious peepers panned the near horizon searching for any indication that their pursuit had been sussed out by the rustlers. It was a nerve-tingling period.

Morgan led the way along the narrow draw which twisted and turned between rocky bluffs as it forged ever deeper into the main bulk of the Grape Mountains. He almost felt like welcoming the relief that an imminent showdown would bring.

But it was not to be. At least for that day. Lengthening shadows were slowly spreading their sinuous fingers across the sandy bottom as the sun disappeared over the western ramparts. The Missourian called a halt.

'We'll pitch camp here,' he said. 'But it'll have to be a cold one. We can't risk a fire being spotted by some eagle-eyed guard.' His broad shoulders lifted in a gesture of regret. 'Sorry folks, but it's water and beef jerky for supper.'

Alice sauntered over to her horse.

'Well then its lucky that I brought along some cold apple pie and candy bars,' piped up a cheery response. She clucked her tongue in mock rebuke while delving into her saddle pack. 'Takes a woman to think of such things.'

Morgan chuckled. 'I'm lost for words. There sure ain't no reply to that.'

A few other delicacies appeared later and helped to make an otherwise weary night far more tolerable. Morgan's wavering doubts regarding the girl's insistence on accompanying him in search of the rustlers were fast disappearing into the stygian gloom of night.

Settling down under his blanket, the ex-gold miner threw a last lingering glance towards his lovely companion. Their eyes met in the ethereal shimmer cast by a hazy moon. Coy smiles and an unspoken accord passed between them, a hint of more to come once their current business was completed.

Morgan turned, a smile on his face as he huddled beneath the blanket. But his thoughts soon turned bleak. Bullets and spilled blood might well be a yawning chasm that could not be surmounted. It was with that dark image that he eventually fell into a disturbed asleep.

They awoke at first light to a chorus of yapping prairie dogs.

The new dawn was shot through with vivid streaks of purple, pink and gold, a superlative tableau from nature's imaginative paintbrush. Beautiful to behold but lost on the three confederates who knew that a desperate showdown was in the offing.

By mid-morning, Morgan sensed that the finale was near. He slowed their pace to a walk, urging caution and clear sightedness.

4

A Cat's Life

'D'yuh reckon we've got enough steers, Rufus?' asked Cactus Jack.

The rustlers were on the far side of the plateau from where they had established their main camp. They were counting the older beasts as the critters were herded into a secluded amphitheatre called Arrowhead Canyon. The boss of the gang and his sidekick were slapping their lariats urging the recalitrant back markers into the fenced-off enclosure.

They had finished altering the Praise B brand on the older steers into what was a more than acceptable alternative. A few deft changes with the running iron had produced a new outfit called the Box 8. Gonzales and the Indian briefly checked each steer to ensure they had been given the new brand.

Once the final longhorn was corraled, the Mexican leapt off his horse and slid the securing poles across the entrance.

The boss of the outfit considered the question posed by his partner.

'Thaddeus Webb reckons he'll take as many as we can supply,' remarked Cahill with a grin. 'All we have to do is fix up a time to deliver them to the army base at Fort Calhoolie. Webb has promised to pay up once I let him have the bill of sale.'

'All we have to do now, then, is brand them calves in the small corral,' added Selman. 'Won't take more than a day then we can move 'em all out.'

Cahill nodded. 'You stay here and make certain the brands on these critters look like the real thing. Them blue bellies have been on hard tack for the last month so they're desperate for a regular beef shipment.' He sucked air through a gap in his front teeth. 'But even they might kick up a shindig at buying stolen cattle.'

'Don't worry none, boss,' Selman replied with forthright assurance. 'I'll give 'em all my personal inspection.' He arrowed a quizzical eye towards the bedroll tied behind Cahill's saddle. 'Where are you headed, then?'

'I need to visit Salida to make certain that our deal with Webb is still on.' His cruel mouth tightened into a hard line. 'And make darned sure that it's for the right price.' The town was a two day ride to the west. 'If'n I leave now, I should be back the day after tomorrow.'

He called over to the other two rustlers.

'You fellas get to work on them calves using the new iron I had made by that blacksmith at Bent's Forge.'

Gonzales uttered a manic chuckle.

'That design. Eet ees a work of art, *patrón*.'

Cahill accepted the acclaim with his usual aplomb. 'Sure cain't disagree with you there, Gonzo,' he simpered.

'Only an agent from the Cattlemen's Association could ever spot that them soldier boys have been stitched up. And it's a dime to a dollar that there won't be none of them guys at the fort.'

Cahill was well pleased with the way that the rustling operation was proceeding. He reckoned another couple of deliveries like this and they could all head south for the winter.

Yes sirree! Things were going real swell. And once that dough in his saddle-bags had been buried in a safe place, he would be able to rest a sight easier while they moved the cattle.

'*Hasta luego, muchachos*!' the gang leader called as he spurred off. 'I'll bring back some bottles of best Scotch whisky for us to celebrate.'

The Indian together with Gonzales then headed back across the flats to their camp and the final spell of branding.

* * *

It was Sam whose warped optics were sufficiently focused to spot a thin tendril of smoke rising from the far side of a low ridge up ahead.

Tethering their mounts, the three comrades crept catlike up to the rim and peered over into the valley below.

And there it was.

The end of the elongated draw had opened out into a broad amphitheatre. Open grazing land stretched away towards a line of broken cliffs on the far side. And immediately to their front were two men. Their backs were turned away as they poked at a fire in which an array of irons were being heated up.

Close by was a criss-crossed z-fence corral containing thirty or more calves that were ready for branding.

All at once, something in Morgan's brain twigged.

His whole body tensed up.

Nerve endings twanged as ogling peepers absorbed the odious sight.

It was as if he was looking at his very own double. And except for the eagle feather poking from his hat, it could have been. But this was no mysterious apparition. It was the hated Black Dog Boone, the Commanche breed who had stripped him of more than his clothes. The Missourian's dignity and self-respect had also been severely denigrated.

And that could not pass unavenged.

'Those are the damned skunks that bushwacked me on the Chavez Salt-flats,' he hissed. 'And that's the breed who stole my duds.'

The victim of the insulting travesty grabbed for the revolver he had been loaned by Clay Bishop. But he never got to draw the weapon. It was the solidly dependable hand of Cock-eyed Sam that stayed the impulsive reaction.

'Not now, sir,' intoned the negro in a gruff whisper. 'This needs thought and careful planning if we are to win back cattle . . . and your honour.'

Morgan struggled momentarily as his brain fizzed and bucked. But Sam's grip was like iron.

Eventually he calmed dawn.

'Yeah, OK! You're right, Sam,' Morgan gasped, his muscles still tight as a banker's billfold. 'I guess we need to do this properly.'

Alice's consoling hand rubbed his shoulder. He looked at her from beneath lowered eyebrows, a sheepish grin offering his regrets.

'Sorry about that,' he murmured. 'Just lost it for a moment.'

'It's understandable after what you've been through at their hands,' she assuaged, massaging the tension from the lean torso. Then, scanning the broad flatland below the ridge, her brow furrowed with concern. 'Didn't you say that four men ambushed you?' Morgan nodded. 'So where are the other two?'

His grey eyes widened.

'The leader, a varmint called Rufus Cahill, must be seeing to the rest of the herd they stole.' Morgan's own pointed gaze scanned the terrain. 'The other fella must be with him.'

‘Maybe they went to Salida to find a buyer,’ suggested Alice.

Morgan nodded. ‘Maybe.’

‘So what we do, boss?’ drawled the black man.

The three comrades lay side by side in silence, each trying to figure out their next move. But time was not on their side. The branding was imminent and the two missing rustlers could return at any moment.

It was Morgan Silver who offered a solution.

‘Those two critters have their backs to us,’ he opined carefully. ‘If’n we leave the horses here and creep down, the scrub will give us plenty of cover to sneak up close enough to get the drop on them.’ He checked the ageing five-shot Cooper, then signaled for Sam to follow him around the edge of a cluster of rocks to their right.

‘What about me?’ inquired a puzzled Alice, scrambling to her feet.

This time it was Morgan who was forthright in his resolve to keep her out of danger. 'We need you up here to give covering fire with that Winchester.' He tapped the barrel of the rifle.

'But I want — '

'No arguments, Alice.' The man's features were locked in a mask of immoveable determination. 'This time you do as I say. Agreed?' Momentarily his stern gaze softened.

The girl's narrow shoulders lifted in acceptance. Then, with a surge of defiance, added, 'But if things go bad, I come a-running.' She held his gaze with her own stubborn intransigence.

Morgan smiled. 'You better believe it.'

Then he was gone.

The pair of stalkers bent low, taking advantage of every vestage of cover afforded by the arid rim of the hidden basin. As they drew ever closer, stealth was essential so as not to alert their quarry. Luck was so far on their side. Gonzales and the Comanche half-breed were focusing all their attention on bringing the irons up to the required heat to produce an effective and permanent brand.

Over to the left, the young steers were nervously milling about. Morgan could not see the older long-horns but knew they had to be somewhere in the vicinity awaiting the deft use of a running iron to alter their own brands.

Smoke from the fire twisted and writhed in the still air. They crept ever closer. Everything was going their way. But at that moment, the Devil decided to throw a mischief potion into the melting pot.

It was a dry twig that gave them away. The crisp snap pierced the silence like a gunshot.

Black Dog was the first to react. An alert perception that had been drilled into him as a young brave surged to the fore. Spinning round, he dropped to one knee and palmed his revolver, the one he had stolen from Morgan. The owner instantly recognized the weapon but his own instincts for survival were now kicking in.

Boone snapped off two shots before the attackers had time to draw their own pistols. But his aim was hasty and they went wide. Both factions now stood their ground. Separated by a distance of no more than twenty feet, bullets flew both ways.

Revolvers from both sides were soon clicking on empty chambers. The briefest of lulls followed as fresh rounds were thumbed into the chambers. Morgan quickly slotted a spare cylinder into the Cooper. It was the 1860 model but was still a useful firearm.

Up on the ridge, Alice cursed her inability to assist. Her allies were too close to each other to manage a safe shot.

A yelp of pain to Morgan's left informed him that his *compadre* had been hit. Sam clutched his thigh and went down. But the injured man was still able to return fire.

A lucky shot removed the Mexican's wide sombrero parting the greasy lank hair on his scalp. His hand reached for the sharp pain creasing his bullet head. It came away slick with his own blood.

The sight was too much for Gonzales. He'd had enough. Dropping flat to the ground, he scuttled backwards towards the safety of a broken lean-to so as to avoid any further injury.

Boone, however, was made of sterner stuff. He threw a scowl of contempt at the cowering Mexican. With his associate playing the coward, the Indian now realized the odds had shifted in favour of the assailants.

Then it happened. Morgan's old pistol jammed. He cursed aloud. Cock-eyed Sam was of little help as his own aim was askew because of the gnawing pain from his bleeding thigh.

The Indian gave a hoot of joy. Here was his chance to finish the gunfight in his favour. Boone leapt to his feet.

'Now I finish what boss should have done on salt-flats,' he howled, raising the Remington. His finger tightened on the trigger.

Morgan Silver was staring death in the face yet again. Desperately he wrestled with the faulty mechanism. But to no avail. In despair, and with no hope of averting the inevitable, he threw the useless hunk of steel at the simpering half-breed.

Boone ducked. As the missile flew over his head, he hawked out a grating shout of triumph. Morgan's own gun, clutched tightly in the Indian's hand, lifted. It was ready to blast its late owner into the hereafter.

But the lethal discharge never came. At least not from Boone's gun.

Observing the Indian jump to his feet, Alice took full advantage of this brief window of opportunity to terminate the conflict. She would only have the one chance. Barely sighting along the octagonal barrel of the rifle, she quickly drew a bead and hauled off.

The first shot took the Indian in the shoulder. He spun round, mouth agape in total surprise at this sudden and unexpected attack. A second bullet finished the gunfight as a fountain of red spurted from a ruptured artery in the breed's neck. He was dead before his body hit the ground.

Morgan just stood there. He was in shock. One minute facing the Grim Reaper's grinning maw, the next given another reprieve. He felt like the cat with nine lives.

Alice rose from her place of concealment with the intention of joining her confederates. Observing the move, Morgan quickly waved her back. Cock-eyed Sam struggled to his feet and hobbled across. Together the two *compadres* clung together trying to still their beating hearts.

But the game was not yet over.

5

Unlucky for Gonzales

There was still Gonzales to be considered. Morgan pushed the injured negro down into the cover offered by a clump of prickly pear. He peered across to the rough huddle of sawn timber leaning against a rocky outcrop.

Nothing moved. But he knew that the Mexican had to be inside.

'You better come out now, *muchacho*,' Morgan spoke up bluntly. 'The fight is over and you lost. So I'm taking you in to stand trial.'

Silence.

Only the cawing of a lone coyote echoed across the bleak terrain.

Gonzales had no intention of being hauled off to face a hefty sentence in the state penitentiary. He cautiously peered out of the rickety shack.

A crafty, scheming brain had thus far enabled the Mexican *bandido* to avoid serving time. He recalled the last time a dangerous situation got out of hand.

That was when he was running with Wild Bat Hendry. The Mexican shook his head. Now that guy was more than just wild, he was crazy in the head. Didn't know when to give up and cut his losses. The gang had ridden into the border town of El Paso one Friday afternoon back in '72. Their intention was to rob the bank.

But the heist had not gone according to plan. Somehow the town had been tipped off. The gang had become trapped inside the bank. Two of the tellers were dead and the situation was bleak.

Gonzales had decided that discretion was the better part of valour. So he had sneeked out of the back door of the bank knowing the whole town was preventing their escape down the main street.

Hendry had refused to show any

common sense. The result was inevitable. He and the other lunkheads had paid the price with their lives. Brave *proscritos* cocking a snook at the law, or stupid *idiotas*? Gonzales favoured the latter. He may have escaped empty-handed, but the wily Mexican was no *idiota*. And he could read men's minds.

This fellow outside was no cold-blooded killer like Cactus Jack or Boone. And that was the trait the Mexican intended to exploit to the full. Black Dog Boone was dead. But Vittorio de Espinosa Gonzales intended to ride away from this debacle with his skin intact, except of course for that slight parting of the hair. And that was a small price to pay for freedom.

'You hear me, fella?' Morgan repeated more firmly. 'Are you coming out or are we coming in?'

Gonzales chuckled gleefully.

'Hold on there, *señor*,' the Mexican called back injecting a note of supplication into the response. 'Gonzales not want to end up dog meat. I come out now.'

Slowly he emerged from the old shack they had been using as a base. Hands reaching skywards, he shuffled despondently into the open.

Morgan stepped forward. Having retrieved his own gun that Boone had stolen together with his hat, minus the eagle feather, he quickly relieved the Mexican of his gun.

Alice meanwhile was attending to the bullet wound in Sam's leg.

Morgan fixed a glacial eye on to the cowering Mexican. 'I'm taking you in, mister,' he reiterated wagging the Remington, 'to stand trial for rustling and highway robbery.'

For the first time, a sly gleam appeared in the Mexican's beady orb.

'I think not, *señor*,' he said quietly, the hint of a smirk creasing his florid visage.

Morgan threw him a puzzled glower. What sort of trick was this greaser trying to pull?

Gonzales continued, unphased by the bleak regard.

'Did I not save you from being killed by Cactus Jack Selman following ambush on Chavez Saltflats? That bad boy would have liked nothing better than to give you a dose of lead poisoning. Only Gonzales was man enough to speak up. Surely that will allow good self to leave here as free man.'

'I appreciate what you did,' averred Morgan acknowledging the Mexican's stance before adding a sardonic addendum. 'Even though I would have died anyways if'n these two guys hadn't come along.' He purposely omitted the crucial incident involving the lark and the rattlesnake. 'But I'm still taking you in. I'll make sure the judge hears of your preventing me getting shot out of hand. That ought to earn you a reduced sentence.'

The Mexican grimaced. This was not what he wanted to hear.

'Not good enough, *señor*,' he drawled.

Then turning his back on the tall Missourian, he began walking slowly towards his horse. Outwardly espousing a confident manner, the Mexican was quaking in his scuffed boots.

'Hold on there,' shouted Morgan. The cocking of the pistol was meant to deliver an ultimatum. 'You ain't going no place.'

Gonzales kept walking. 'You not shoot poor Mexican in back,' he said in a flat monotone tinged with nervous trepidation. 'Rufus Cahill is *hombre* you seek. It is he who has your money. A deal was struck to sell cattle to the Top Dog Trading Company in Salida.'

Morgan gritted his teeth. So he had been right all along.

Alice Bishop gasped when she heard the declaration. So T. D. Webb was behind all this rustling. It all began to slot into place: the undercutting of prices; the derisory offer to buy out the Praise B.

And when they refused to play ball, the skunk decided to acquire stolen cattle at a knockdown price and then sell them to the army for top dollar.

Well next time the Praise B would be ready for him.

The Mexican sensed that his revelations had struck home. He took full advantage of the lull. Mounting up he swung the animal away, still keeping a wide back to his fuming opponent.

But Morgan knew he was right. No way would he ever consider shooting a man down in cold blood, and especially in the back. And there could be no denying that without the Mexican bandit's intervention, he would now be strumming with the angels. Or stoking the fires of Hell. It would have been a close run thing as to which way his luck ran.

Nonetheless, he was still miffed. Recovering his ranch deposit now seemed a whole lot more difficult.

Gonzales disappeared round the bluff. A huge sigh of relief issued from his fleshy lips. His intention was to leave the territory and start up again elsewhere. Digging his spurs into the cayuse, he pounded off in the direction of a soaring finger of rock.

* * *

Riding back from the hidden canyon to join his partners, Jack Selman was startled by the flurry of gunfire. He dragged his mount to a halt. It was coming from the direction of the main camp. That could only mean that some cowpokes had discovered their trail.

As luck would have it, the penned steers were located on the far side of the bluff. That meant he could not be seen by the attackers. However, with only Boone and the Mexican left to brand the new calves, Selman realized he would have to do something, and quick, if this sticky situation were to be turned around. At least he would have the advantage of surprise on his side.

The hard-boiled rustler kicked his mount back into motion and veered away to the right. Selman's idea was to gain a high vantage point amidst the chaotic array of boulders. From there he could observe the camp from the far side of the rocks and decide what needed to be done to regain the upper hand.

Scrambling up to a point where he could look down on the scene of conflict, the outlaw was shocked to witness Boone lying in a pool of his own blood. He was clearly dead as a doorpost. Another dude lay on the ground holding his leg. A cowpoke was holding a gun. From that distance it was impossible to pick out the guy's features. For some reason he just stood by watching as Gonzales mounted up and rode away.

Selman scratched his neck. A puzzled grimace soured his leathery features. Why had they let him go? Had that two-bit chiseller struck a deal and blabbed everything?

Any notion of fair play did not register with the cold-blooded Texas gunman. Back-shooting was easier than facing down an adversary every time. There was only one way to find out whether Gonzales was running out on his partners, or escaping to warn the absent Jack Selman.

Sliding down the back slope at the rear of the bluff, he quickly mounted up and headed to the far end of the line of cliffs where the trail divided. Going left headed round to where they had left the older steers. But skewing to the right would mean the greaser was quitting the scene altogether.

Selman growled. Nobody ran out on the gang.

Either way, from where the gunman was intending to lie in wait, he would be able to cut him off. Swerving between clumps of mesquite and sagebrush, he spurred the hardy mustang to a frenetic gallop across the flat plain.

Ten minutes later he arrived at a large stack of red sandstone jutting from the sandy wasteland. Nailed to the base of the towering pinnacle known as

Bianca Butte, was a faded sign. In red paint, an arrow pointed west to Salida, south to Raton Pass and the New Mexico border.

He was only just in time. The pounding of hoofs assailed the gunman's ears. Gonzales hove into view. He reined in peering at the signboard. A moment's hesitation, then he swung the horse's head to the right.

An ugly snarl hissed from between Selman's clenched teeth. He grabbed his pistol, emerging from cover to block the traitor's path.

Taken by surprise, Gonzales reined to a stumbling halt. Ogling peepers fasten on to the ugly snout of his one-time buddy's revolver.

'You in a hurry to get somewhere, *amigo*?' smirked the hardcase gesturing for the Mexican to dismount.

Gonzales's mouth flapped open like a landed pike, but nothing emerged. He was dumbfounded.

'I guess you didn't hear me.' A hard edge had crept into Selman's challenge.

'Where are you going in such an all-fired hurry?'

'I-I . . . was going for help . . . to find you, Jack,' stammered the Mexican trying desperately to sound confident. 'Cowboys attack us, kill Boone. I only manage to escape by skin of teeth.' A hesitant smile hoped to appease the grim-faced outlaw whose cold regard now held him in a grip of steel.

'That so?' Selman replied with a mindful nod of the head. He appeared to relax, a loose smile cracking the granite features. But it was all a charade. 'Then how come you took the trail for the New Mexico border, you double-crossing skunk?' He didn't wait for an answer. 'You were running out on us. That ain't a healthy option . . . *amigo*.' He laid a heavily sarcastic emphasis on the final word. 'Not healthy at all.'

'Is not so,' blustered Gonzales, his pleading look receiving a scornful glower. 'Gonzales would not desert *compadres*.'

Selman racked back the hammer of his Remington-Ryder. Then, a slight hesitation flickered over the brutal contours of his face. If he shot the Judas, it would alert the cowpokes. The terrified Mexican saw the wavering indecision. He turned around and ran for the cover of some nearby rocks.

But too much indulgence in lazy living had made him corpulent and slow. Short stubby legs waggled as he struggled to escape the inevitable.

A harsh laugh pursued him.

Selman holstered his pistol and dragged a heavy knife from the sheath attached to his right boot. Flicking it so as to catch the blade between his finger tips, he launched it in a single fluid motion at the lurching form. Even a blind man couldn't miss such a broad target.

The lethal blade struck the Mexican in the middle of the back. Arms flailing wildly, Gonzales pitched forward on to his face. Not yet dead, he struggled manfully to drag himself into the shelter of the nearby rocks. It was the feeble gesture of a dying man.

Selman ambled over and jabbed his boot into the broad back.

'Too late, *hombre*,' he sniggered. 'You took the wrong trail.' Then he bent down and heaved out the dripping blade wiping it on the Mexican's greasy head. A final gasp and the Judas lay still.

Selman smiled to himself. Now he could get rid of those interfering cowpokes. A row of buzzards perched atop the adjacent bluff. Their strident cacophany matched the leery guffaw as the hungry predators eyed the tasty treat. The killer strolled back to his cayuse and checked the loading of his Henry carbine. Mounting up he headed back in the opposite direction to that of the unfortunate Gonzales.

As he neared the scene of recent bloodshed, the rustler paused. He dismounted and scurried back up to the rim of a low bluff overlooking the camp. Removing his high-crowned hat,

Selman scanned the battleground.

There were only two cowpokes present. The rustler screwed up his eyes for a better look. One was a black dude, and he was clearly wounded. Closer now than previously, the other jigger looked suspiciously familiar. Then he turned around.

Selman's gaping mouth registered shock.

It was that jasper they'd robbed on the saltflats. A low growl escaped from between gritted teeth. One more reason to have snuffed out that greaseball Mexican. Somehow the guy must have gotten free and reached the safety of the Praise B ranch.

But Selman was not concerned. With the black man out of action, he should have no difficulty removing this lucky cuss once and for all. He cursed. If only he hadn't exchanged that long-barrelled Sharps hunting rifle for the Henry back in Cripple Creek. The latter was a repeater but lacked the range of the older Sharps.

Too late for recriminations now.

The only option was to move forward and catch the skunk unawares.

Gingerly, the rustler crept down through the scattering of boulders. His quarry was bent over the injured man trying to dress the bullet wound. More important, he had his back to the killer.

Selman cat-footed into the open, pistol palmed and cocked. Relishing the decisive advantage of surprise, he could have just hauled off. But Cactus Jack had always preferred to make an overt display of his intentions. It was the fear of death etched into the stricken faces of his victims immediately prior to the final blackout that gave him a huge kick.

'Turn around slow and easy, mister,' he rapped out. 'And don't try any funny business.'

Morgan's whole body tensed. He recognized that ugly snarl. Slowly he stood up, arms raised, and swung on his heel.

'I figured you would have gone with

Cahill to look after that dough.' He paused, struggling to contain his anger. 'My dough!'

Selman laughed. 'Not any more. And you ain't gonna have the chance to spend it anyways. Say your prayers, lunkhead, cos your luck just ran out.'

His finger tightened on the trigger.

A shot rang out. The piercing report propelled a desert hare out from beneath a lone yucca. The terrified animal streaked across the open ground into the rocks so recently vacated by Selman. Birds launched themselves into the still air.

Cactus Jack teetered then reeled backwards. Clutching hands reached for his chest where a large red splodge quickly blossomed.

A lithe shape slowly rose from the low hill behind clutching a Winchester. It was a stroke of luck that Alice had gone back to retrieve their horses from below the rim.

Even from a distance of two hundred yards, Morgan could see that the girl was trembling. He hurried towards her as she staggered down the rough slope. Without a thought, he encircled her in his strong arms, kissing and stroking the wavy locks of red hair.

Alice luxuriated in the powerful security of the man's protective embrace. The blood of two men on her hands in less than an hour was enough to weaken the stoutest of hearts.

Tears flowed. No words were spoken. A gentle soothing from Morgan slowly eased away the shocking brutality of the episode. Together, they continued over the far side of the hill so that Alice would not have to witness the results of the conflict at close quarters.

Then Morgan returned for the injured negro.

The stolen herd would have to be collected by Praise B riders, the nearest of whom would likely be at the far end of the north range. It was a sad rather dispirited trio that headed back down the draw.

A successful conclusion to their

mission, perhaps. But the harsh reality of cattle ranching in the valley of the Arkanas River left much to be considered.

6

Salida

The injury sustained by Cock-eyed Sam proved to be superficial. The bullet had only creased his thigh. It looked a sight worse than it was. After three days of loafing in the bunkhouse, the tough negro was itching to get back into the saddle. Only at the firm insistence of his feisty young charge did he condescend to rest up until fully recovered.

More relieved to have the three hunters back than the return of his stolen cattle, Clay Bishop offered up a prayer to his Maker beside the grave of his beloved wife. Martha had been taken by an outbreak of cholera three years previously almost to the day.

Clay had laid her to rest in a quiet corner of the ranch behind the main house. Beneath the leafy shade of a cottonwood, he had planted beds of columbine and larkspur. In this tranquil setting the rancher and self-proclaimed minister prepared his sermons.

And that was where Morgan found him.

Like Sam, Morgan was also chafing at the bit. Although his own impatience stemmed from the desire to seek out his enemy to recover the stolen money. If Gonzales had been telling the truth, then he would find Rufus Cahill in Salida. And there was no valid reason indicating that the Mexican had been lying.

Standing on the outside of the small cemetery, Morgan waited for the rancher to finish the passage he was reading from the Good Book. His bedroll and saddle-bags were packed.

When Clay Bishop saw him, he knew straight away that the younger man was intent on leaving to pursue his quest of vengeance. He just hadn't thought it would be so soon. He fully understood, and sympathized. In the same position he would have done the same.

Nevertheless, the rancher cautioned the young frontiersman against following the road of violent retribution.

'I ain't gonna try to stop you,' he said. 'All I ask is that you don't do anything foolish. T.D. Webb is a slippery customer and he's gathered some tough varmints to back him up. If a settlement can be negotiated by talking, then I urge you to follow that course of action.'

'Don't worry about me,' Morgan stressed firmly. 'I ain't about to put my head in the lion's mouth. I just want to suss things out before deciding how to make my play.'

Bishop nodded. 'Glad to hear it,' he sighed. 'All the same, I'd feel a heap better about things if'n you'd take one of the hands with you. He can pick this month's supplies up in the wagon and watch your back at the same time.' The rancher thought for moment. 'Will Tennant is good man. Handy with a gun but no hothead.'

'Much obliged to you, Clay,' replied Morgan, hestitating. 'Fact is, old Sam has been pestering me to let him mosey along. The guy reckons he needs to look after me.' His eyebrows lifted meaningfully. 'Can't say as I blame him. Although it was Alice that saved us both from lead poisoning.'

'That young lady just won't settle down. It worries me no end, I can tell you.' The rancher's broad shoulders slumped, the concern etched into the leathery skin of his face. 'A woman shouldn't oughta be handling guns the way she does. Makes me feel awful nervous. All the same, I can't reprimand her for saving your bacon, can I?' The brief feeling of melancholia lifted as he added with a warm smile. 'The gal sure has taken a shine to you. And I ain't about to chastise her for that neither.'

Morgan blushed. 'Sh-she does s-seem to have cottoned on to me,' he stammered. 'Can't think why.'

'Maybe when this business of your'n

is settled, you'll consider helping me rub some of the edges off'n her. Turn her into a real lady and not some kinda wayward tomboy.'

'Well I . . . I don't know about that.'

Bishop gave the stumbling reply a half smile before his face reverted to a pensive frown. 'Is Sam up to riding yet?'

Morgan shrugged. An audible sigh of relief escaped from between clenched teeth now that he was back on safer ground. 'Don't see why not. It'll probably do him more good than mooning about the ranch kicking his heels all day.'

At that moment, the man in question hove into view around the side of the barn. He limped across. The awkward gait was assisted by a stick. Morgan noted, however, that Sam did not appear to be in any pain from the injury.

'My left ear is hotter than the desert wind,' observed the negro cowhand rubbing at the said appendage. 'Some'n tells me that you guys have been talking about me.'

'Howdy there, Hoppy.' Morgan aimed a wry smirk towards the ranch boss. 'You all set for earning some pay after your vacation?'

'Umph!' The object of the quip speared them both with an erratic look. 'Any time you are,' Sam countered, tossing the stick aside with a cavalier gesture.

'Then let's ride.'

Morgan was glad that Alice had decided to visit her friend Bridget McCabe over at the small town of Fairview where she ran a haberdashery store. If the girl had been mindful of his decision to go after the stolen money, like as not she would have insisted on tagging along. And that was a distraction towards which he had no hankering.

* * *

Drawing his mount to a halt on the outskirts of Salida, Morgan cast a wary eye over the huddle of buildings. Log cabins predominated with a scattering of pitch-pine false fronts along the main street. An untidy plethora of shacks and corrals had grown up behind. Grubby white canvas tents scattered around gave the town a transitory air of impermanence.

But one building stood out from all the others. It had been erected on a raised terrace behind the town. Painted white it boasted a sturdy wooden cross. Adjacent was a small cemetery. This must be the church where Clay Bishop presided on Sundays, except when he was otherwise engaged. On those occasions, another preacher came in from Fairview to conduct the services.

However, the structure that really caught Morgan's attention was situated at the far end of the street. A large double storey building, the name of the establishment was garishly painted in red and gold lettering. Morgan stiffened when he read it.

Top Dog Trading Company.

So that was where Rufus Cahill had thrown in his lot. And doubtless the stolen two grand was locked up inside a safe there as well. His hackles rose. Every sinew of his being screamed out to gallop down the street and challenge the varmint to a showdown.

The ever reflective Sam appeared to read his bubbling thoughts.

'T.D. Webb has a bunch of tough gunslingers on his payroll. You be sure and take it slow and easy, Mister Morgan.'

The advice received a curt nod. He knew that his partner was right. No sense putting his life on the line until he was holding all the aces.

'I'll put out a few feelers in the saloon,' he said. 'Where should we meet after you've picked up the supplies?'

'How about Ma Baker's Cowboy Cookhouse?' suggested Sam. 'That gal makes the finest son-of-gun-stew you ever tasted. Maaaaaan!' he drawled. 'My taste buds is plumb watering just thinking on it.'

'Suits me,' concurred Morgan nudging his mount forward.

He tugged his hat down to ensure the taut features remained in shadow. Only Cahill could recognize him. But the critter might even now be eyeballing every stranger who rode into town.

Morgan Silver didn't know how close he had come to sussing out the truth.

In his office on the second floor of the *Top Dog*, Thaddeus Deakin Webb stood before the window puffing on a large cigar. He was surveying Salida's main thoroughfare when his beady eyes narrowed to thin slits.

Cock-eyed Sam stood out like a sore thumb. Since the end of the Civil War, freed slaves had drifted west seeking work on the burgeoning cattle spreads. Most had headed for Texas. Thus far, only a handful had settled in Colorado. Sam was the only one that Webb knew of working in the Freemont Basin. And he was employed by that interfering Bible-basher, Clayton Bishop.

He threw down the smouldering

cigar butt and viciously ground it into the carpet with his boot heel. An accusatory finger stabbed at the cowpoke who was hauling the wagon to a halt outside the general store at the far end of town. It was a rival establishment run by the McCluskey brothers.

Six months previously, Buff and Sean had sold up their cattle spread in New Mexico and come north. Salida had offered exciting prospects for a permanent establishment. They stocked everything that day-to-day living demanded. And reasonable prices had ensured their success.

Then T.D. Webb and his gang had arrived.

Within weeks the newcomer had set up in competition and begun undercutting his rivals. However, the bonhomie of the jovial Irishmen was enough to retain the loyalty of most of their clientele. Seeing that cheaper prices were not working, Webb ordered his men to threaten the miners who frequented the store.

A few cracked skulls and broken bones were sufficient inducement to punch a serious dent into the McCluskey profits. The affable brothers would have been forced to sell up at a knockdown price had not Clay Bishop come to the rescue.

A firebrand preacher, he had urged the local cattle ranchers to resist the roughshod tactics of the Top Dog from the pulpit of his church.

'Bishop has sent that damned cotton-picker to buy his supplies from the McCluskeys,' he snarled at the other occupant of the room who was idly picking his fingernails with a knife. A balled fist hammered the wall. 'I told them skunks what would happen if'n they carried on trading against me.'

The other man pushed himself off the wall and casually peered out of the window. He shrugged. This was no business of his. All Rufus Cahill was concerned with was selling the rustled cattle to the army at Fort Calhoolie.

He threw a sneering look of disdain

at the merchant's back. His hat was the latest from the Stetson company. Four new ones had been delivered the previous week. The store-bought suit and ruffled shirt must have cost a pretty penny as well.

Such adornments held no allure for the outlaw. Leave all that fancy stuff for guys like Webb. Cahill had other ideas for his dough.

He smiled to himself, his devious mind drifting away. The two thousand from that hick prospector plus the money from the cattle sale would give him enough to set up a decent sized spread. And with his own brand — the Box 8, the sooner the better.

'You listening to me, mister?' rapped Webb when he did not receive any conciliatory response.

'Sure, sure, TD,' Cahill assured the ranting businessman while idly glancing out of the window. 'It ain't right. Some'n oughta be done about them bogtrotters.'

Webb grunted, his wide forehead

crinkling. 'The slave has brought along some back-up as well.'

At that distance and with his hat pulled down, there was no chance of Cahill fingering the man who he reckoned had long since hit the Alleluia Trail. He looked away. The rustler was anxious to get back to camp and drive the stolen herd to the fort.

'I'll be headin' back to the valley,' said Cahill moving away from the window. 'Them steers will be branded and I wanna get them on the move.'

Still muttering to himself over by the window, Webb impatiently waved the rustler away without acknowledging his departure by way of the back door.

Morgan was half way down the main street. His eyes flicked from side to side seeking out any potential danger. A loose hand rarely strayed far from the gun on his hip.

'Howdie, stranger.'

Morgan's back straightened. His head shot back revealing taut features in the afternoon sun. Swivelling round in the saddle, he silently cursed as the same light glinted on a tin star.

Tubb Ricketts was seated outside his office in the shade beneath the overhanging veranda. The sheriff was a short stocky dude who had seen better days. Once a tough enforcer of the law in such boom towns as Abilene and Hayes City, he was now seeing out his remaining years in the backwater of Salida. It was a far cry from the rip-roaring excitement of his youth. But that's how Tubb preferred it.

'Ain't seen you around these parts before.'

'I'm just passing through,' answered Morgan. 'Helping out on the Praise B for a spell to raise me a grubstake.'

'That so,' mused Ricketts who had levered himself out of the chair and was now giving the tall stranger an even shakedown. Something was bugging him about this guy. He took a step forward, focusing on the rider's face. 'We met some place else, fella?'

he questioned. 'Abilene, maybe, or Dodge?'

Morgan shrugged. He'd never set eyes on the guy before.

'No matter,' mumbled the sheriff. 'All the same, we run a quiet town here. So just keep outa trouble and you'll be mighty welcome.'

'Much obliged, Sheriff.' Morgan re-set his hat to shade out the prominent features. 'A couple of beers then I'll be heading back to the ranch.'

He swung away. Pointing his horse to the far side of the street, he tied up at the hitching rail. Sam was nowhere to be seen. No doubt he was in the store of the opposition further down the street.

A final look behind as he mounted the steps of the boardwalk brought a puzzled expression to the tanned visage. That nosey sheriff was still skewering him with an evil eye. He shrugged off the uneasy feeling. Tin stars were all the same when a stranger rode into their bailiwick.

But this was no random appraisal from Tubb Ricketts.

The sheriff had seen that face before. But where?

Scratching at the stubble on his jutting chin, he thought deep and hard. A niggling itch was telling him that this guy was not what he purported to be. And Tubb Ricketts had always found that it paid to heed these hunches.

Then his eyes bulged wide. He clicked his fingers as the dime dropped.

For a man of his bulk, the sheriff could move remarkably fast when the need took him. In the bat of a gnat's eyelid he was back in the office searching through a pile of Wanted dodgers gathering dust in the bottom drawer of his desk. The dog-eared collection was of criminals who had escaped the legal net but were still active.

Tubb had always made a point of checking them each month. His earnest endeavour had now paid dividends.

He soon came upon the one he sought.

A pudgy finger jabbed at the head and shoulders of the pen drawing.

'Yessirree!' came the fervid exclamation.

No doubt about it. That was Snakeskin Bob Petrie with whom he had just been jawing. And the jasper was worth a cool two thousand bucks — dead or alive! Tubb's share of the reward would be five hundred. His eyes lit up.

Grabbing a shotgun from the rack, he thumbed in a couple of cartridges and then checked his revolver. He peered out of the window. Petrie had disappeared inside the Jack Rabbit saloon.

A year had passed since Tubb Ricketts had faced down a wanted killer. That had been up north in Cripple Creek. And on that occasion, he'd slugged the guy from behind giving him no chance to retaliate. The Montana Kid had netted him a couple of hundred.

Tubb's flaccid jaw tightened, grey eyes clouding. This guy was a far more serious proposition. He dug into his desk and pulled out a bottle of hooch. A couple of liberal slugs to steady his nerves and he was ready.

7

Arrested!

Inside the shady portals of the Jack Rabbit, Morgan was ordering a beer. He threw a casual eye over the saloon's clientele. The usual array of afternoon drinkers were present, none of whom paid the newcomer any attention.

A gambler idly shuffled his deck awaiting the start of the evening session. At the far end, a game of billiards was in progress. Two cattlemen were discussing the price of beef.

After serving the newcomer, the barman continued polishing glasses.

'Is there a bank in this town?' Morgan asked. 'Didn't see one as I rode in.'

'You got money to deposit, then the Top Dog is the only safe place,' replied Carl Hegglestein. Morgan's eyes lit up.

The bartender didn't notice his customer's sudden interest. He was only too eager to have somebody fresh with whom to converse. 'T. D. Webb has one hefty mother of a safe in that office of his on the first floor. The only problem is that he charges you interest for the privilege.'

'Doesn't sound like a good investment to me,' said Morgan.

Hegglestein nodded. 'We tried persuading the Colorado National to open a branch.' A baffled frown wrinkled the guy's forehead. 'They seemed keen enough at first.' He paused shaking his head.

'What happened?' Morgan pressed.

The 'keep responded with an oblivious shrug.

'Nothing. We never heard back from them. Can't figure it out. This town could go places with a proper bank.'

'Maybe this T. D. Webb character convinced the bankers that Salida wasn't a good place to set up.'

Hegglestein placed a finger to his lips.

'That kind of talk is likely to get you into trouble, mister,' he hissed. 'Others have voiced their suspicions and paid the price.'

'How d'you mean?'

'I've said too much already,' mumbled the bartender sidling away. 'Just drink your beer and talk about the weather. It's a whole lot safer.'

Morgan got the message loud and clear.

The Top Dog was just the sort of place to which a skunk like Rufus Cahill would be drawn. He was now satisfied that his money was in that safe and earning Webb interest for every day it remained there.

The tall Missourian was hunched over his glass musing on how best he could get that dough back when he got the shock of his life.

'That sure is a mighty fine hatband, mister.'

The gruff remark was like a slap in the face to the unwitting drinker.

'The only other one I ever saw like

that was on the wanted dodger of a killer named Snakeskin Bob Petrie,' continued the lawman's icy censure. 'It wouldn't be you would it, fella?' Ricketts didn't wait for a reply. 'Now turn around slow and easy. And keep them mitts well away from that hogleg. The state's offering a hefty reward for you, Bob . . . dead or alive. Take your pick! Cos it don't matter none to me.'

Silence descended over the saloon as all eyes focused on the showdown being played out at the bar. Dust motes floated effortlessly in the beams of sunlight filtering through the glass of the front window. Nothing else moved. But only for a brief instant. Suddenly, chairs slammed back as patrons sought to remove themselves from the line of fire.

Tubb Ricketts alone stood rooted to the spot.

Feet planted square, back straight, the old lawdog was back in Abilene. Lethal scattergun in one hand, revolver in the other. Just like old times.

As if in slow motion, the accused man swung on his heel.

Ricketts nodded towards a sheet of paper resting on the bar top.

'Take a look, mister,' he spat out. 'And tell me you ain't that murdering sonofabitch. Then I'll call you a goddamned liar.'

Morgan's gazed dropped to the sheet. He was lost for words. After all this time, he figured the trail would have gone cold. He'd grown a moustache and changed his name.

He cursed his stupidity for keeping the hat. Even after Black Dog Boone had stolen his duds, that was the one item he'd felt the need to repossess.

'I have a way where faces are concerned,' smirked Ricketts gesturing for one of the ogling drinkers to remove the prisoner's holstered gun. 'Once seen never forgotten. Don't matter to me that you've grown that handlebar, put on weight or even taken to wearing spectacles. The face don't change.'

The lawdog was enjoying himself.

This was going much better than he could have hoped.

Ricketts then addressed one of the drinkers. Luke Breckenridge was often deputized when the lawman had to leave town. 'Fetch this guy's gun and bedroll over to the hoosegow. And don't take your eyes off'n him for a second until he's locked up tighter than Belle Starr's corset.'

'Do I get to wear a badge?' exhorted the eager assistant.

'Sure you do, Luke,' breezed the sheriff full of his own importance at having collared a wanted villain. 'And you're on the payroll until the sheriff of Green Ridge arrives to take this fella back there to stand trial. I'll go send him a wire right now.' Ricketts arrowed a warning glare towards his new deputy. 'Sure you can handle this, Luke?'

'Don't you worry none, Tubb,' enthused the proud deputy. 'I've got the jasper covered.'

The sheriff reacted with an assured nod before continuing.

'This guy sure is one wily critter to have escaped the long arm of the law for this long.' He gave a throaty laugh, pointing his gun at the wanted man's hat. 'Wearing that piece of fancy headgear didn't do him any favours,' he said to the room in general. For the disconsolate prisoner, he reserved a disdainful sneer, 'But you sure as hell met your match in deciding to stop off in Salida, didn't you, Snakeskin?'

Morgan Silver, alias Bob Petrie, remained tight-lipped as he was ushered through the door of the saloon.

Once the trio had exited the fusty, smoke-filled parlour, talk broke out as everyone offered their opinion as to the identity of the killer so recently in their midst.

While the lynx-eyed Luke Breckenridge prodded his stunned captive towards the jailhouse, the sheriff hustled across to the telegraph office. And a reminder would be included in the cable for the arresting officer to bring the reward money.

Tubb figured that if the local lawman in Green Ridge set off immediately, the guy could reach Salida in less than a week. The train from Denver would drop him off at Canon City. A steady ride due west across the Cotopaxi Plateau by way of Freemont Pass would then see him in Salida within four days.

This unusual degree of animation on the main street of Salida had attracted a host of onlookers. It wasn't everyday that a wanted killer was apprehended in the town. The last time had been a year before when Shotgun Harvey Nixx and his gang had tried to rob the assay office.

Charley Packer had been sheriff at that time. He stood his ground in the middle of the street and gunned down the leader as he tried to escape. Like headless chickens the rest of the gang had scarpered leaving the sack of stolen money lying in the street. Charley had received a near-fatal bullet in his right lung. It had effectively terminated his career.

This arrest had been a sight less hazardous.

Among the bystanders was Cock-eyed Sam. After leaving Morgan, the negro had gone directly to the McCluskey store and given the Praise B list to Buff McCluskey. He was enjoying a welcome chinwag with his brother over a mug of coffee laced with a generous measure of Scotch when a passing miner clattered through the door.

'A wanted killer has been arrested in the Jack Rabbit,' he announced in a breathless rush before departing.

The guy's assertion was supported by a welter of loud voices and running feet hustling past the store window. Everybody was running in the direction of the saloon. The two brothers hurried outside to ascertain the source of the hullaballoo.

Sam's jaw dropped on witnessing his partner being frog-marched over to the jailhouse. What had the guy done in so short a time to have stirred up such a hornet's nest? There was only one way to learn the truth.

'Get my stuff packed in the wagon, Buff,' he said to the storekeeper. 'I have to see what this is all about.'

'You know that dude, Sam?'

'He's been staying at the ranch,' replied Sam while keeping a steady gaze on the progress of the bizarre turn of events. 'Is a long story. And I ain't got time for the telling just now.'

The negro cut across the street and down a narrow alley. His aim was to approach the hoosegow from the rear. The cellblock backed on to a small corral where he hoped to be able to contact the prisoner once he had been incarcerated.

Nobody was around. Most of the town's citizens were out front watching the unexpected though welcome diversion to their mundane lives. Sam ducked down behind a line of water barrels. And waited.

Five minutes passed before the rattle of keys accompanied a squeaking of rusty hinges as a cell door was dragged open.

'Make yourself at home, Snakeskin,' chuckled a muted voice from within. 'You best enjoy this five star accommodation at the town's expense while you can. The law'll be here inside of a week to take you back to Green Ridge. Then you can dance a jig at your very own necktie party.'

A whistle meant to convey a degree of churlishness followed. Sam held his breath, ears atuned to every nuance of the virulent diatribe.

'Two thousand bucks has to make you a perty important *desperado*,' snorted the jailer. 'And remember, the dodger says dead or alive. So you'll be well advised not to try any funny business.'

A loud guffaw echoed through the barred window of the cell. It was followed by a slamming of the door and the retreat of footsteps. Another door closed as Deputy Breckenridge returned to the front office.

Sam was totally baffled. Green Ridge, Snakeskin, Wanted dodger? Who was this guy that he had helped rescue and come to regard as his friend? His mind was in a turmoil. He waited a further five minutes before venturing out from his place of concealment.

Creeping over to the thick adobe wall, Sam peered around to make certain there were no voyeurs. A wooden crate enabled him to step up level with the barred window of the cell.

'Mister Morgan!' he hissed. 'That you in there?'

A shuffling told him that the cell's occupant had heard him.

'Sam?'

'What in tarnation have you gotten yourself into, man?' Exasperation was clearly evident in the cowpoke's sharp retort. 'Who in thunder is Snakeskin? And what's this about the law in Green Ridge?'

Further questions could have poured forth. But the cock-eyed negro was lost for words. He just couldn't believe that the dude he had helped bring back to life from the Chavez Saltflats and accompanied on a mission to reclaim rustled cattle was nought but a wanted killer.

The ensuing silence crackled with tension.

Sam's quizzical tone brought the whole sorry episode back into sharp focus.

8

The Past Catches Up

Bob Petrie had laboured long and hard for the small amount of gold he carried in his saddle pack. His claim was located fifteen miles north of the boom town of Green Ridge. High in the bleak wilderness of the Mummy Range, the narrow ravine's one claim to eminence was that it lay at the source of the mighty Colorado River.

While panning the cold water that eventually poured out into the Gulf of California, such geographical titbits were the last thing on any gold seeker's mind. Locating the shiny paydirt was all that mattered.

The nearest settlement was at Timber Creek, but it was little more than a trading post. Those prospectors who wanted to exchange their hard-won lucre for dollars had to brave the arduous three day trek through the mountains to the nearest assay office at Green Ridge.

The rider gave a sigh of relief when the town hove into view. He removed his hat dragging a weary arm across his sweating brow. Without thinking he flicked the tail bones poking from the diamond-shaped skin that encircled the hat making them rattle. Whenever he was questioned about the odd habit, he claimed it brought him luck.

It was this practice that had led to the young prospector being nicknamed Snakeskin.

Being early afternoon with the sun at its most virulent, most citizens were indoors taking a rest from the incessant heat. In consequence, the main street was empty. Petrie nudged his horse down to the far end where the assay office was to be found. It was set apart from the rest of the huddled structures that made up Green Ridge.

Hogwart Halliday had specifically

chosen this quiet site so that no passerby could eyeball the valuable commodity with which he dealt. The relative isolation of the office was both an advantage, and, as Bob Petrie was about to discover, a major handicap.

He drew to a halt beside the small log cabin and dismounted. Entering the front office, the harsh glare from the sun was abruptly blotted out. It took some seconds for his eyes to become accustomed to the gloom. That brief interlude was enough for all hell to break loose.

A shot rang out.

The blurred form of the assay agent sank to the dirt floor. Before Bob had chance to gather his wits, the killer dashed across and cracked him over the head with a pistol. Stunned, but still conscious due to the tough material of his hat, Petrie made a grab for the burly assailant.

Another brutal slug took him down but he had managed to grasp the varmint's shirt. The worn cloth ripped down from the shoulder. The last thing Bob Petrie saw through his rapidly clouding vision was a purple birth mark. Boldly striking, it was etched into the killer's left forearm in the distinct shape of a five pointed star.

That was the last thing he saw before keeling over.

Close by, Hogwart Halliday lay in a spreading pool of blood. His days of assessing the value of gold dust were well and truly numbered.

No more than five minutes could have passed before Petrie regained his senses. He struggled to his feet rubbing at the growing lump on his head and desperately trying to recall what had occurred. It had all happened so fast.

His pained features creased as he tried to recall the details of the attack. There had been a gunshot. The assay agent was being robbed. Then he had been knocked cold. As his vision cleared, watery eyes fastened on to the dead body.

That was when the door burst open

and two men ran in.

'Don't you dare move a muscle, fella,' snarled the elder of the two who was brandishing a lethal shotgun, 'else I'll cut you in half with this here blaster.' Sunlight, spearing in through the open door, glinted on the polished metal of a lawman's badge. 'Now drop that gun and step back.'

Petrie swayed on his feet. His gaze lowered to the revolver clutched in his meaty fist. It was a .44 Smith and Wesson, nothing like his own pistol which was an 1863 Army Remington converted to cartridge loading.

'This ain't my pistol,' he blurted out dropping the weapon like it was a red hot poker. 'I didn't kill Halliday. Some other dude had just robbed him when I came through the door.' More than a hint of panic registered in the cracked assertion. 'You have to believe me. I'm innocent.'

The faces of the two lawmen remained flat and icy cold. They were totally unmoved by the despairing plea.

Deputy Chad Fuller carefully secured the fallen pistol and sniffed at the warm barrel. He nodded towards the sheriff.

'It's been fired recently. And my bet is that the bullet dug out of poor old Hogwart is a .44.'

'My figuring too,' concurred Sheriff Cab Garrety. 'I'm arresting you, mister, for the willful murder of Hogwart Halliday. The circuit judge is due in town next week. So we won't have long to wait for the trial.'

'And it don't look good,' added Fuller with a mocking shake of the head. 'Hogwart was well liked around here. He allus paid out fair and square. The jury ain't gonna be too disposed towards his killer. My bet is they'll be calling for a quick hanging.'

Petrie was stunned. 'But it wasn't me,' he stressed. 'The skunk you want has got away and left me holding the can.'

'Save it for the trial,' barked Garrety quickly snapping the steel cuffs on to the hands of the tottering captive. 'It ain't me you've gotta convince, its Judge Tyler.'

'And they don't call him the Hanging Judge for nothing,' added a smirking Chad Fuller.

An abrupt push sent the accused man sprawling out on to the street where a crowd had gathered.

'Make way, folks,' hollered Sheriff Garrety. 'This varmint just shot and killed Hogwart Halliday.'

A discordant murmur rose up into a swell of anger.

'Why don't we just hang him now,' shouted an irate bystander.

'Yeah!' hollered another. 'We don't need no trial. There's a handy tree over yonder.' The crowd surged forward.

Garrety pointed his shotgun into the air and loosed off one of the barrels. The raucous blast halted the mob in its tracks. In a flash he had palmed his new Colt Peacemaker.

'There'll be no vigilante law in this town while I'm sheriff,' he growled in a low yet penetrating rasp. 'First man to take another step forward gets the other barrel.' Dark hooded eyes panned the sea of faces. When nobody made to challenge the lawman's blunt threat, Garrety stepped down into the street. 'In that case, there's nothing here to keep you. Go about your business and let me get on with mine.'

Still nobody moved.

'D'you critters hear me?' he hollered waving the shotgun. 'Skidaddle afore I lose my temper.'

'You heard the sheriff,' snapped Fuller pushing forward to add some much needed support. 'Clear the street now before somebody gets hurt.'

Slowly the tense gathering began to break up. Groups of disgruntled men shuffled away deep in conversation. The panic was over, for now. But Garrety was in no doubt that he and his deputy would have to stay fully alert until Judge Tyler arrived.

And that couldn't be too soon.

Bob Petrie was locked in the cell at the rear of what had once been a sawmill. The solidly built edifice was the only stone built structure in the town. It had grown up on the edge of Shadow Mountain Lake. Dense stands of pine encircling the broad amphitheatre had encouraged Pitchpole Jarvis to set up in business.

That had been ten years before.

Jarvis had left when the ground became too steep for easy access to the trees once the lower slopes had been stripped bare. An ugly patch of stumps was all that remained.

Green Ridge prospered as gold seekers flooded into the Upper Colorado valley. And with them came the usual denizens hoping to grab their share of the new bonanza. Territorial law finally superceded the loose-knit amalgam of miners' courts. These drumhead convenes tended to pass judgement without due regard to proof of guilt.

As Garrety and his deputy surveyed the slowly emptying street, the sheriff pondered on the fact that such a primitive means of maintaining order had not been fully eradicated.

It was going to be a long week before Judge Tyler arrived.

The sheriff was not the only one who was worried. Petrie had been present when other vigilante courts had been in session. Little in the way of proper legal procedure had been adhered to. If that mob got itself liquored up enough, anything could happen.

And so it came to pass.

Later that night, the mob returned. This time they had burning torches and plenty of guns. The prisoner was awakened by the blood-curdling howl of the baying mob. He could hear Garrety trying to calm them down. But he was having little success. It could only be a matter of time before they overpowered him and broke into the jail.

Desperately, Petrie looked around his cell. The window was solidly barred, as was the door. He was trapped.

Then a flickering eye settled on the fireplace.

An idea suddenly blossomed in the dismayed prisoner's mind. He hustled over to the empty grate praying that the chimney had not been barred over. Lying on his back, he stuck his head into the hearth and peered up the flue. A palpable sigh of relief followed. It was clear, if somewhat on the narrow side. But there should be enough room for a lythe guy such as himself to shimmy up and then make his escape.

Without further ado, he discarded his heavy coat and vest. The all-important bag of gold dust was hung around his neck. Then he began worming his way into the constricted apperture. The vengeful howling outside lent impetus to his fateful endeavours: his very life was at stake. At least with a trial, there would have been a chance to plead his case. But a frenzied mob was not about to ask any questions as they dropped the noose around his neck.

Soot and flakes of dislodged ash cascaded down the chimney. It settled in every crevice and orifice. Choking and wretching, the climber kept slipping back when the old stonework collapsed under his weight. The tiny gap of moonlight never seemed to get any closer. With every muscle straining, Petrie forced his aching body upwards. Cracked and bleeding fingernails scrabbled for holds.

Then suddenly, his head felt the cool breeze of the night air. One last heave and he was out on to the sloping roof of the jailhouse. On all fours he edged along the ridge shingles aiming towards a flat section one floor below.

But some lynx-eyed drunk had spotted him.

'There's the murderin' critter up on the roof.' The strident bellow rang out attracting the attention of all the others. Flaming torches waved as a bellowing rage erupted from one hundred throats.

'He's tryin' to escape!'

'Gun the bastard down!'

All attempts to break into the jail were forgotten. Here was their quarry. And he was about to wriggle out of their clutches. A hail of bullets spat from rifles and pistols as the mob desperately tried to prevent the prisoner evading vigilante justice.

Petrie ducked down on the far side of the roof as hot lead pinged and zipped off the stone chimney. Scrambling crab-like along the slanting pitch of the roof, he hurled himself on to the flat lean-to at the side. Screwing up his aching peepers, Petrie looked down to the back lot behind the jail.

His luck was in.

A saddled horse was standing immediately below his position. Without thinking he jumped into the blackness trusting that his momentum was accurate. Landing with a solid thwack in the saddle, the startled horse reared up on its hind legs emitting a frightened whinny.

The fugitive dug his heels into the flanks of the cayuse which bounded forward just as the leading members of the wailing horde hurtled round the edge of the jail. More gunfire erupted pursuing the fleeing escapee. But only a lucky shot would have brought the absconding rider down.

Hugging the neck of his mount, Petrie spurred the horse to a full gallop. Soon he had been swallowed up by the impenetrable gloom.

* * *

'You listening to me, Morg — or whatever your name is?'

The stifled hiss resurrected the dire situation in which Bob Petrie now found himself. He shook out the fog that threatened to envelop his stunned brain. Yeh! Bob Petrie was now Morgan Silver, or was, until that Wanted poster had leapt up and bitten him on the ass.

'It's all a question of mistaken identity,' stressed the confused prisoner. 'I've been accused of robbing an assay office and killing the agent. But I didn't do it.' He quickly filled the negro in with an account of the unsavoury episode finishing with an urgent plea.

'The sheriff has wired Green Ridge for the lawman up there to come and get me. He'll be here soon now there's a railroad link to Denver.'

He had only just finished the grim exposé when the door to the cellblock creaked open.

'Who's that you're talking to in there, back-shooter?' Luke Breckenridge rapped sticking his head into the corridor, a Spencer carbine in plain view.

'Only trying to work things out in my head,' said Morgan injecting the reply with a wheedling tone of resignation.

'Save it for the jury in Green Ridge,' ordered the preening deputy who was thoroughly enjoying his moment in the limelight. 'According to a second wire that's just come down the line from Sheriff Garrety, only a miracle is gonna save you now.'

A mumbled grunt was the sole reaction to this bleak testament.

'You hear me, boy?' rapped Breckenridge. He didn't wait for a meaningful reply. The slamming door propelled a harsh guffaw down the corridor.

'You can see what I'm facing, Sam,' whispered Morgan. The insistent entreaty was not lost on the black man. 'You gotta help get me out of here so's I can prove my innocence.'

After listening to the bizarre tale, Sam was in a quandary. He sure wanted to believe the guy's avowal that he was telling the truth.

'How do I know you ain't come down this neck of the woods to pull off some other robbery?' The submission was hesitant, uncertainty etched into every syllable. He didn't know what to think.

A dog's strident barking interrupted the dialogue. It was quickly followed by a gruff curse. Sam ducked down behind the barrels. But nobody appeared. He waited a moment before scrambling back up to the window.

'I'm heading back to the ranch now,' he declared firmly having reached a compromise with his bewildered conscience. 'The boss will know what's best.'

'OK. Guess I'll just have to put my trust in your good judgement.'

The response was listless, devoid of enthusiasm. Yet in truth he couldn't have expected anything more from the stolidly dependable negro. The poor guy had been handed a poisoned chalice and didn't know whether to drink the elixir or throw it in the dust.

'Just remember that sheriff will be here in little over four days. Let's hope that Clay can figure out something before then, otherwise I'll be dancing at the Devil's elbow for durned sure.'

9

A Cunning Plan

The ride back to the Praise B was uneventful.

Sam constantly tossed the recent revelations over in his mind, assessing the freakish situation from every angle. His head was buzzing like a nest full of wasps when the wagon finally trundled into the corral fronting the main house of the Praise B.

He had kept up a relentless pace not stopping for a rest other than to relieve himself. The deadline for rescuing the prisoner was etched starkly in his thoughts.

If the guy was indeed innocent, then time was of the essence.

Other hands working on the ranch paused in their tasks. Curious eyes pondered on the hurtling wagon as it ploughed to a halt in front of the porch in a cloud of dust.

Without bothering to acknowledge their presence, Sam hustled up on to the covered veranda and rapped hard on the solid oak door. Within seconds the Chinese cook answered the door.

Lee Fong's head bobbed. He stepped back as Sam rushed into the hallway.

'Where's Mister Clay?' he shouted earnestly. 'I gotta see the boss now!'

The Chinaman just stood there, his mouth agog, stunned into silence at this unexpected display of consternation from the normally placid negro.

'Is that you. Sam?'

Not waiting for an answer, Clay Bishop skipped down the flight of stairs that dominated the entrance hall. For a guy in his late fifties, he moved with the supple grace of someone half his age. The thick shock of iron grey hair barely moved an inch as he came to a halt before the sweating negro.

Neither did he display any hint of anxiety. Clay had long since learned to control any outward sign of distress when others around him were panicking. It had always given him an edge.

'So what are you so all fired up over?'

'It's that guy what calls hisself Morgan Silver,' the negro blurted out waving his long arms round like a windmill. 'He ain't that at all. And seems like he could be a murdering robber as well . . . '

Bishop held up both hands to curb the ex-slave's galloping fulmination.

'Hold on there, Sam.' he chastened. 'Just calm down. Let's you and me discuss this over a pot of coffee in the den.' He turned to address Lee Fong. 'And bring us some of them fresh-baked billberry muffins as well.'

The cook bowed and hurried off while Sam followed his guardian into the ranch office, ubiquitously known as the den.

'Now you slow down to a steady plod,' mollified Bishop laying a comforting hand on the agitated negro's shoulder. 'And tell me everything that has happened since you and Morgan left for Salida.'

It was a protracted hour later that the narration reached its timely conclusion. Clay only posited an odd question here and there when some point needed clarification. Other than that he allowed the negro a free rein.

A silence of around five minutes followed as the rancher digested the startling events. He selected a long-stemmed pipe and stuffed it with tobacco. Lighting up, he puffed on the briar while strolling up and down the room. The action always helped to concentrate his thoughts.

'Four days, eh? And that's now been reduced to three.' Bishop was talking to himself, mulling over the options. 'In your considered view, Sam,' he said fixing a stoical eye on to his adopted confederate, 'is this Snakeskin Petrie on the level? Has he been wrongly accused?'

Sam's left eye rolled in its socket as he gave the request due thought and deliberation. He'd thought of nothing else since the visit to the jail.

'I reckon he has, boss.' His reply was measured and firm in its conviction.

'Then it's our bounden duty to rescue him from the hangman,' announced Bishop who had likewise arrived at the same judgement. A plume of thick blue smoke accompanied the announcement. 'Can't have an innocent man go to the gallows while the real killer roams free, now can we?'

Sam offered a vague burble of accord. A palpable sigh of relief whistled from between clenched teeth now that the responsibility for such a momentous deduction had passed out of his hands. He was not used to shouldering such heavy burdens.

With the boss in full agreement, he was certain that all would be well.

'And this is what we're going to do — '

'I hope you guys aren't intending to cut me out of this caper.'

The soft tones jerked the two men from their earnest discussion. Both heads turned towards the svelte figure standing in the doorway. So intent had they been in thrashing out the details of how the rescue of Morgan Silver was to be conducted that they had failed to heed the girl's presence. Alice had arrived back from Fairview the previous evening.

'How long have you been listening in, girl?' rapped her father. 'This is private talk and no concern of your'n.'

'Well that's where your wrong, Pa.'

Hands firmly planted on her shapely hips, Alice faced the two men square on. Her resolute stare was irrefutable. She eyed them both with a fierce determination not to be sidelined.

'Wasn't it me that found Morgan in the first place, then nursed him back to health? And didn't I save him and this skallywag?' A smirking thumb jabbed at the stunned negro. 'Both of them would have been gunned down in cold blood when we thwarted the rustlers but for me.'

There was no denying either contention.

But Clay Bishop did not want to put his only daughter in further danger. For he knew that the proposed plan was fraught with all manner of pitfalls. Busting a prisoner out of jail was a man's job. Failure would inevitably lead to a long spell in the slammer, or even a booking with the Grim Reaper.

All these solid reasons washed over the girl's straight back like hot butter off a knife. She was not to be moved.

'I'm in and that's final,' she stated flatly moving into the room. 'Now let's get the plan worked out.'

Bishop shrugged, raising his hands in surrender. Rolling eyes sought accord with his sidekick. But Sam remained neutral. His flickering gaze shifted between father and daughter. This had to be their decision, not his.

* * *

It was dawn the following morning. The sun was peeping above the scalloped moulding of the Grape Mountains to the east. Streaks of vivid pink and mauve scored the heavens like a flurry of loosed arrows. It was a sight to behold as the party of three men and one female trotted under the longhorn gateway fronting the Praise B holding.

In addition to the boss, Cock-eyed Sam and Alice, they had recruited Jimbo Dawson to give the rescue team a mean-eyed appearance. The cowboy was the oldest hand on the ranch apart from the boss. Nobody knew his age. Somewhere between forty and sixty had been banded about. The craggy face had the appearance of a crumpled brown paper bag, much of it hidden by a thick grey moustache.

He had served with Captain Bishop as his sergeant in the 3rd Ohio Infantry during the war. Following the cessation of hostilities, they had remained together. Jimbo had become an accepted part of the Bishop family's endeavour to carve out the new frontier in the western territories. As ramrod of the outfit, Clay trusted the grizzled veteran with his life.

To all intents and purposes, Alice looked like a youthful cowhand in her range gear. She had deliberately rubbed dirt into her smooth face to lend authenticity to the disguise. Her father had to admit that she looked the part. Complete with holstered Colt Lightning and battered Stetson, nobody would realize she was anything other than a trail-weary deputy sheriff.

For that was the subterfuge Clay Bishop was figuring to pull off.

Passing himself off as the Green Ridge lawman, he hoped to fool Tubb Ricketts into releasing the prisoner into his custody. To achieve that, they would need to reach Salida before the real escort arrived, then disappear into the surrounding landscape.

The previous day had been spent preparing official looking documentation authentic enough to pass for the real thing. Alice was the ranch bookkeeper. Once the spread had begun to prosper, a small press had been purchased for printing off ranch documents related to bills of sale, purchase orders and a host of other authoritative records that a thriving business demanded.

Clay was pretty sure that what he now had in his possession would do the trick. He had no qualms regarding any of his escorts being recognized. Ricketts had only been appointed to the sheriff's job the month before, following the previous incumbent's untimely demise.

Rumour had it that Trampis Filbert had balked at taking orders from the Top Dog Company. A broken neck when he was discovered down a ravine was adjudged to have been an unfortunate accident.

Ricketts had supposedly been recommended by one of T. D. Webb's business associates in Denver.

Sam was the only rider who was likely to be recognized. Not only due to his unique appearance, but because of the recent visit to the town for supplies. It was, therefore, agreed that he should wait on the outskirts in case something went wrong and back-up was required.

They approached Salida from the north east, the direction from which Cab Garrety would come.

Clay drew them to a halt in a clump of cotton-woods a half mile from the town. He hooked out his Hunter pocket watch and flipped open the lid. It read 5.08 in the early evening. Time enough to conclude their deception and make a clean getaway under cover of dark.

'This is it then.' announced the rancher.

All four pinned on the tin stars that had been fashioned by Jimbo who also acted as ranch blacksmith. Bishop sucked in a large gulp of air to calm himself. A rising tangle of nerves was fluttering in his stomach now that the moment of truth had arrived. Once they rode out into the open, there would be no turning back.

'You stay here, Sam. And keep them cock-eyes peeled for the real escort.'

'Sure thing, boss.'

'They aren't due until tomorrow.' he added. 'But if'n Garrety does turn up early, you're gonna have to figure some way to delay him.' He fixed a salutary peeper on to the solidly dependable black man. 'You OK with that?'

'Don't you fret none, boss,' the negro concurred tapping his pudgy snout expessively. 'Old Sam has a few tricks up his sleeve from the plantation days to throw any pursuers off the scent.'

'Figured you might have.' Bishop gave the nervous quip a tight smile before jogging away into the gathering shadows.

10

Subterfuge

The rancher led the way as the trio drew near to the first of the buildings that hugged the outskirts of Salida. Alice rode behind with Jimbo Dawson bringing up the rear and leading a spare horse for the released man.

The bogus escort's arrival in Salida had been purposely gauged to coincide with the onset of evening. That way, Bishop could be sure that nobody would recognize them. Grey fingers of approaching dusk blurred the edges of reality as the three riders entered the outer limits of the town.

At that time of day, few people were about.

Only then did Clay notice the plume of smoke rising above the other buildings. A few yards further and the full horror of the scene struck home.

'Ain't that the McCluskey place?' posed Jimbo.

The store was now just a heap of smouldering ash. The charred bones of the once thriving business lay scattered in ugly disarray. And seated on the front step were the two brothers. Their whole dream had gone up in smoke.

Clay bunched his fists. This had to be the work of Thaddeus Webb. Clay felt a pang of guilt. It was his fiery sermons that had encouraged the smaller land-owners not to be browbeaten by the Top Dog into abandoning the brothers. Now this!

Much as he would have liked to offer the McCluskeys a helping hand, this was neither the time nor the place.

'We can't do anything for them now,' he said sensing the indignation of the others. 'Maybe once this business is concluded, I'll offer to tide them over until the insurance comes through.'

Not wanting to be recognized, the rancher steered his mount down a side street. He had to quickly shrug off the recent shocking revelation. All their concentration had to be focused on convincing Tubb Ricketts to release his prisoner. Nothing else could impinge on that result.

With that thought in mind, his intention was to approach the jail from the rear just like Sam had done. That way they could be certain not to attract any unwelcome attention.

Tying up within the small corral, Clay ordered his associates to wait there while he conducted the business within.

'Be ready to ride as soon as we return,' he said keeping his voice down to a choked whisper. 'And keep them hoglegs palmed and ready . . . just in case there's trouble.' His final comment was to his headstrong daughter. 'And if there is gunplay, I want you to promise me that you'll keep your head down and stay out of it.'

Alice was about to offer some boisterous rejoinder. But her father got in first with a blunt demand.

'Promise!! Otherwise we pull out now and forget this whole charade.'

There was no way that the rancher was going to put the life of his only kin at risk for anyone. No matter who.

The girl was initially stunned by the emphatic mandate. But she immediately recognized her father's serious intent. His dark eyes bored into her, urging a conciliatory reaction.

'You got my word, Pa,' came back the firm yet compliant assurance.

'Then wish me luck,' Bishop said gripping Jimbo's gnarled hand which was followed by a brief hug for his daughter.

'You won't need it, old buddy,' the ramrod exclaimed forcing his gnarled features into a twisted grin. 'A guy like you could sell snow to the Eskimos.'

And with that final chortle ringing in his ear, Clay disappeared around to the front of the jail.

A firm knock on the door was followed by a terse command to enter. Bishop breathed deep, then opened the door. A blast of hot air from the potbellied stove hit him. It was still early April so the heat of day soon dispersed after sundown.

Bishop coughed in preparation for the dialogue he had prepared.

'Are you Sheriff Ricketts?' he spat out curtly.

'Who wants to know?' came back the equally suspicious reply.

The lawman was slumped in a seat and had not yet noticed the badge adorning his visitor's vest. A half empty bottle of tequila was clutched in his hand. The burning down of the McCluskey store had unsettled him.

Ricketts had urged caution on the scheming crook. But that had not prevented Webb from carrying out his threat. The sheriff had gone along with it just so long as the conflagration could be explained away as an accident. A hefty bonus to his pay packet had helped appease his conscience.

'Sheriff Cab Garrety from Green Ridge,' shot back the newcomer. 'Here to collect a prisoner. My escort is waiting outside round the back.' He removed a document from the inside pocket of his sheepskin coat and handed it over.

That sure got Ricketts' attention.

'I wasn't expecting you until tomorrow,' he gulped.

'We made better time than expected,' replied the bogus lawman.

Ricketts grunted as he studied the release order. Then a frown creased his blotched cheeks. 'This ain't the normal form of release far as I can recall,' he challenged thrusting out his stubbled chin. 'Fact is, it don't look nothing like the one handed over when I collected Blacktail Frank McGraw from up that neck of the woods.'

Bishop was ready for the controversy. He had been hoping that the document's official appearance would quash any dispute. Nonetheless, his response was well rehearsed.

'I know what you mean, Tubb.' The bogus lawman coughed out a brisk guffaw. 'New council members are always wanting to stamp their brand on a town once they get elected. This is the new mayor's doing. You know how it is.' He shrugged as if to say, what could a humble officer of the law do about it.

Tubb nodded his understanding. 'Guess you're right at that. So,' he continued rubbing his hands together, 'once you've handed over the reward, I can sign the release. And then, the critter is all your'n and we can drink to a job well done. Got me some some mighty fine Scotch in the drawer.'

Reward?

This was something Clay had not foreseen. Ricketts must have wired the Green Ridge sheriff to bring it along. Struggling to maintain a straight face, the rancher slowly curled his lip into an expression of regret.

'Unfortunately, that's another problem with new officials.' He shook his head. Hands outstretched in apology, a look of disappointment clouded his face. 'They just ain't trustin' enough. I tried to tell him. But the mayor insisted that this varmint is delivered to Green Ridge before he'll authorize the handover of any reward money. I sure am sorry, Tubb. But there ain't a thing I can do about it.'

Ricketts fumed. What should he do? T.D. Webb was waiting on his major cut of the reward as they spoke. The Top Dog boss would be none too pleased at this development.

But if Tubb refused to release the prisoner, there would be no money anyways. He would have to go along with this guy's orders.

'OK,' he drawled acidly. 'Its a deal. Don't reckon I have much choice in the matter. But I want it in writing that the two grand will be sent down by special courier as soon as you get back to Green Ridge.'

Bishop gave an inner sigh of relief.

'You got my word as an honest lawman,' he said offering a prayer to his Maker for the blatant deception.

They shook hands and the form was duly signed.

Tubb went through to the cellblock.

'On your feet, Snakeskin,' he ordered with a mirthless chortle. 'The escort's here to take you to your very own hangin' picnic.'

The prisoner shuffled out of the cellblock. His feet awkwardly dragged the ball and chain across the floor. It was an extra security measure insisted upon by T.D. Webb. Head sunk on to his chest, weary eyes stared at the wooden floor. Morgan had given up all hope of a rescue. Sam had clearly not believed his story.

'Don't reckon we'll be needing them,' announced the bogus sheriff briskly. 'My deputies'll make sure this jasper don't try to escape.'

The prisoner's whole body tensed. Could it be? Slowly he raised a sceptical eye. The tough, resolute face of Clay Bishop stared back willing him to maintain a deadpan look. It took all of Morgan's resolve to control his facial muscles and prevent them giving the game away. Only a slightly raised eyebrow betrayed the elation coursing through his veins.

As Ricketts bent down to unlock the fetters, Clay winked at his associate. Morgan allowed himself a brief smile before settling back into the despondent mien expected from a condemned man.

'Well, he's all yours, Cab,' concluded Ricketts accepting the signed receipt and affidavit that the reward money would be sent as soon as possible. 'Where you spending the night?'

'Figured we'd hit the trail,' replied Bishop escorting his prisoner back down the corridor to the door at the rear of the jailhouse. 'Make camp in a couple of hours. We don't want to waste any time getting back to Green Ridge and that trial, now do we? Sooner this critter is fitted with a tailor-made hemp scarf, the sooner you'll have your dough.'

Ricketts gave an eager nod of accord.

'Sure I can't tempt you with that Scotch?'

'Best not,' replied Bishop. 'Gotta keep a clear head for this guy.'

Rickett's shrugged. His thoughts were already trying to work out how best to appease Webb. The hard-nosed trickster would not be well pleased at having to wait for the lucre.

Not a single word was uttered as the uneasy group of riders made their way back to the cottonwood copse where Cock-eyed Sam was anxiously waiting. Sharp ears were atuned for any unusual sound, in particular the sudden clamour indicating that the deception had been rumbled.

But only the heavy sough of their own breathing cut through the oppressive silence. Otherwise, total darkness enfolded the landscape. When they reached the rendezvous, an unexpected surprise awaited them as they drew rein under cover of the cluster of trees.

Sam had been joined by the McCluskey brothers.

'These two fellas came by whilst you were . . . ' He paused not wishing to reveal the true reason for his mysterious presence on the edge of Salida.

'Yeah!' interjected Clay. 'We saw them down the street aways.' Then addressing the two forlorn Irishmen, he said, 'Seems like you had one heck of an accident in the store, boys. Any idea what caused it?'

'Ricketts tried to claim it was our fault,' replied Buff McCluskey in a disgruntled voice.

His brother Sean then took over. 'He mouched around some then came up with the notion that a spilt barrel of coal oil must have come in contact with the stove and set the place on fire.'

'Load of hogwash!' railed an irate Buff. 'We always make sure to store the oil well away from any source of heat.'

'So what d'yuh reckon caused it?' butted in Alice Bishop.

'That lowlife skunk, T.D. Webb, has to be at back of it,' growled Buff McCluskey. 'He threatened us with some kinda retaliation if'n we didn't sell out to him at a rock-bottom price.'

'We told him where to stick his miserly offer. Now we won't get anything. The store's a heap of smouldering debris.'

'And we didn't take out any insurance,' added the morose Buff.

Following this revelation, a brief period of tense reflection followed. The momentous implications of the brothers' outpouring needed some digesting.

It was Clay who finally offered them a lifeline.

'It ain't much to offer you guys,' he said, 'but the Praise B can sure use some extra help at this time of year with the branding. I aim to play Webb at his own game and sell my beef at a lower price direct to the army. But I need more hands for the trail drive to Fort Calhoolie, guys who can use a shooter, in the event of retaliation by that skulking backshooter and his gang.' The rancher gave the two brothers a serious look. 'You fellas up for that?'

The faces of the two brothers lit up.

'That's mighty decent of you, Mister Bishop,' replied an upbeat Buff McCluskey. He looked at his brother. Sean nodded. 'We'd both be more than obliged to accept.'

'Then there ain't nothin' more to keep us hangin' around here.'

Jimbo Dawson couldn't resist a sly dig in the ribs of their recently freed partner. 'You can say that again, buddy.'

Only the McCluskeys remained blank-faced.

'I'll fill you in once we get back to the ranch,' chuckled Clay Bishop spurring off.

'Yehaw!' hollered an over-eager Jimbo Dawson.

'Keep it down!' the rancher ordered gruffly. 'We ain't out of the fire yet.'

'Sorry about that, boss,' came back the contrite reply. 'Just got a mite too fired up.'

Once clear of immediate danger, Morgan drew his horse level with the rancher to voice his gratitude. And surprise at the manner of his escape.

Clay Bishop accepted the heartfelt appreciation with a curt nod. But his stiff bearing revealed a terse reticence.

'You done well by me when you went after them rustlers,' he said. 'But Sam here's been telling us about this business up in Green Ridge.' He fixed the younger man with a focused regard. 'And that needs some explaining away. I've laid my reputation in the hands of the Lord for you, mister. I only hope it's been well deserved.'

'I told Sam and I'm telling you, Clay.' Morgan laid a heavy emphasis on his declaration. 'I was framed for that robbery. It was some other critter that done it. And the skunk got clean away leaving me to take the blame.'

Both men held each other's gaze; one searching for the truth, the other an acceptance of his plea. A night owl hooted in the distance. Bunched clouds were nudged aside by a glistening moon, its silvery glow capturing the tense atmosphere as the rancher pondered over the dilemma.

'My heart tells me that you're telling the truth, boy,' iterated the stoic rancher. 'My head says that I'm a durned fool. Fact is' — he paused to gather his thoughts — 'I've always played my hunches right down the line. It served me well in the past. Let's hope I ain't been caught out by a sucker punch with this one. You're on the team, Morgan. Or is it Bob Petrie?'

'Until I can clear my name,' replied the relieved fugitive, 'reckon it's for the best if'n I stick to being Morgan Silver.'

'And I second that.'

The female rejoinder to his left almost unseated the rescued man. He had noticed the other riders but hadn't given them much attention. The sheer joy at having escaped the hangman's ministrations had been at the forefront of his thoughts. Eyes widened as he tried to probe beneath the dust-caked exterior. A set of gleaming white teeth grinned back at him.

Removing her hat, Alice shook out her long flaming tresses.

'Think I was about to let these pesky galoots have all the fun?'

The blithe remark broke the tense atmosphere.

Sam clapped the wanted man on the back. 'Sorry I harboured any doubts,' he drawled. 'Now let's ride.'

'Think nothing of it . . . partner,' grinned Morgan.

Slapping leather, the riders urged their mounts into a steady canter away from the scene of the recent escapade. A feeling of muted elation at having successfully accomplished a dangerous undertaking settled over the small group of riders. The McCluskeys had a different reason for their gratitude.

Yet, at the time, none of them could have foreseen how much the venture was going to provoke a stunning recoil in the none too distant future.

11

No Luck for Garrety

It was mid-afternoon of the following day.

Thaddeus Webb was becoming more aggrieved by the minute. That sheriff from Green Ridge had arrived mid-morning. He had stayed a half hour then ridden off with his deputies, but without taking his prisoner. And he hadn't returned since. The gang boss had posted lookouts to report on any unusual movements.

All that morning had been spent with his lawyer drawing up deeds for the piece of real estate on which the McCluskey store had stood. Webb intended to build a dance hall and saloon on the site. Then he would make the same offer to Carl Hegglestein of the Jack Rabbit.

By the end of the year, the unscrupulous swindler intended to have a monopoly over all trade in Salida. Under his management, the Top Dog Trading Company was destined to become the biggest commercial enterprise in the territory. Things had been looking good.

Until today.

The first downer had been the arrival of Rufus Cahill announcing that his men had been shot dead and the rustled Praise B cattle had disappeared. And now this unsettling business at the jail.

'Where in thunder is that lunkhead Ricketts?' he bawled, slamming his chair back and looking out of the window for the fifth time in the last hour. 'He should have let me know what's going on by now.'

Webb grabbed a bottle of Scotch and sunk a hefty belt. He didn't expect an answer to the brusque query. And the three other men in the room had no intention of voicing any opinion. The boss was best left to stew when he was in these moods.

Only Rufus Cahill remained indifferent to the bombastic outburst. He was equally disturbed. But for different reasons.

All he wanted to do was ride out after the skunks who had killed his partners and stolen what he deemed were his cattle. After all, hadn't many of them been stamped with the Box 8 brand on their haunches?

But he needed the backing of the Top Dog now that he was on his own. Without their guns he was powerless. All Cahill could do for the time being was wait, and hope they would back his hand. After all, Webb stood to gain substantially once the steers had been sold to the army.

Much to his consternation, Cahill now had an additional reason for paying a visit to the Praise B ranch. One that he sure didn't want any of these critters discovering. The ruthless outlaw had reckoned the incident in

Green Ridge was buried in the past. Now it had come back to haunt him.

The killer had always assumed he had gotten away scot free after robbing the assay office. Being able to put the blame squarely on the shoulders of that poor sap who had intervened was a stroke of luck. He didn't know Petrie had escaped, always assuming the guy had been convicted and hanged. Now he was free again. And doubtless would be seeking revenge.

Cahill's one big advantage was that nobody knew it had been him who committed the offence. That long-ago night had been dark and the guy had not seen his face.

Nevertheless, the rustler could barely conceal his irritation. Only when he'd got rid of this thorn in his side could Rufus Cahill move on. And it would be a long way from this godforsaken dump.

Over by the window, Webb's eyebrows met in the middle. Something was wrong. He could feel it in his bones.

Why hadn't that starpacker left town with his prisoner?

'Ricketts is coming across the street, boss,' called Mace Honniker, a mean-eyed hardcase from Amarillo. 'Looks like he's heading this way.'

Webb growled. 'Well he had better have some good news.' He slammed the bottle down hard. The men shuffled their boots, throwing wary glances at one another. 'I pay that jigger to solve problems, not create them.'

A few minutes later, the hesitant tread of boots sounded in the corridor. They stopped outside the office. There was a tentative knock on the door.

'Come in!' Webb hollered. 'Don't just stand out there wettin' your pants.'

Ricketts edged into the room, hat in hand. The hunted look pinching his red cheeks was all Webb needed to know.

'What in blue blazes has gone wrong?' he snarled. 'All you had to do was release one prisoner and collect the reward money.'

'It wasn't my fault,' whined the

harrassed lawdog shaking his head. 'He had the right sort of document and sure acted like a real sheriff.'

Webb threw him a bewildered look of contempt. What was the bastard talking about? He raised his hands cutting off the burbling flow.

'Hold it right there,' he rasped. 'You best explain what has happened. And don't leave a blamed thing out.'

It took the better part of a half hour to wheedle, coax and browbeat the entire sorry episode from the reluctant mouth of the Salida lawman. It did not make for an edifying disclosure.

'I'm sorry, TD, but how was I to know that — '

'Shut your trap and let me think,' butted in the fuming gang boss as he strutted up and down the room. 'You've done enough damage already.'

'So who could this fake sheriff be?' posed Dallas Biglow, a Utah ruffian.

Cahill allowed himself a private smirk. He could have told them. But he kept his knowledge well under wraps.

'Has to be someone from the Praise B,' shot back a belligerent T.D. Webb. 'I saw this killer with my own eyes arrivin' in town. He rode in with the blackie who works for Bishop. Couldn't be anyone else.'

This time Cahill couldn't contain his impatience.

'Then what we waitin' fer. Let's hit the trail,' he urged levering himself off the wall. 'We can burn that ranch out, kill this critter and claim his reward, and then drive them cattle to the army post at Fort Calhoolie.' He looked around for support. The other hard-cases remained silent. They were only paid for their gunslinging prowess.

'You're right, Cahill,' agreed Webb. 'No sense hanging around any longer. That sheriff has quite a start. So we ain't got time to lose. Get your gear together, boys. We ride in half an hour.'

* * *

'Riders coming in off the south range, boss.'

The sudden announcement came from Canute Larsen. The blond-haired Swedish cowhand had been tending the vegetable garden that was his pride and joy. He had earned the nickname from the infamous king who had tried to stop the tide coming in. Larsen similarly had an aversion to sand invading his revered plot of land. He continually swept it away.

Bishop hurried over to the front window of the house. Emerging from the cloud of dust, he picked out three horsemen. None of them were from these parts and the leader was wearing a shiny tin star.

Ever since the release of Morgan Silver, the rancher had come to realize the seriousness of what he had engineered. No way could he hope to get away with such an audacious deed indefinitely.

And here was the proof of that deduction.

He was now glad about having insisted that Alice go back to visit her friend in Fairview. Cock-eyed Sam had accompanied the girl to ensure that nothing happened along the way. Clay wanted her well clear of the ranch should any trouble break out.

'Looks like that sheriff from Green Ridge has come a-calling,' voiced the rancher. 'You stay here, Morgan, while I send him on his way.' He winked at the younger man. 'I have a very persuasive manner when its needed. That posse will be crossin' the New Mexico border afore figuring out they've been hoodwinked. And by then you'll be long gone.'

Morgan replied with a stiff nod. He had come to the same conclusion. There was no future for him on the Praise B, or with Alice. Cut his losses and light out. Best for all concerned, not least his benefactors.

He watched the stiff-backed rancher stroll across the front yard to greet the posse. He was accompanied by Canute who was carrying a shotgun.

'Howdie there, Sheriff,' he breezed,

pasting a forced smile on to the rugged face. 'What can I do for you boys?'

The lawman who stared back was less than cordial with his own reply.

'Are you Clay Bishop of the Praise B ranch?' he said in a frosty tone.

'That I am.' The rancher cleared his throat struggling to hide his unease. 'And who might you be?'

'Sheriff Cab Garrety of Green Ridge in the Upper Colorado Basin.'

'Is there something wrong?' queried Bishop.

'I have reason to believe that you are harbouring a wanted felon on these premises by the name of Snakeskin Bob Petrie. He was recently assisted in an escape from the jail in Salida by a trickster posing as me.'

Observing the nervous reaction of the Swede, the two deputies fanned out so as not to present an easy target to him or any watching bushwackers.

'And you figure it was me?' huffed Bishop, eyes wide and full of surprised incomprehension. 'That's a crazy notion.

Ain't I been here all week, Canute?' posed the rancher of his sidekick.

'You not move from ranch,' concurred the big Swede. 'I vouch for that.'

'And who's been accusing me of this low-down crime?' railed the indignant rancher drawing himself up to his full height of six feet two. 'Somebody who has to be jealous of my success, that's for sure.'

'It don't matter none who passed on the information,' snapped Garrety. 'If you've nothing to hide then you won't have any objection to me searching the premises, will you?'

Bishop's response was a languid shrug as he gestured for the posse members to go where they pleased. He had no other choice. He could only trust that Silver had made himself scarce, otherwise . . . '

Fifteen minutes later, they returned empty handed, much to Bishop's relief.

'Fact is, Sheriff,' said the rancher. 'That just reminds me. It clear slipped my mind. A couple of guys did call in here only yesterday. They asked to water and grain their mounts before heading south for the border with New Mexico. Said they were headed for Cimarron.'

That snippet of information had Garrety listening intently.

'That's mighty interesting, Mister Bishop. I'm obliged to you.'

'Think nothing of it, Sheriff.' The rancher was feeling a whole lot easier having convinced the lawman to head off on a wild goose chase. 'Some folks in these parts can't stand seeing a guy make some'n of himself.'

'*Adios*.'

Buenos Días,' replied Bishop as the three men rode away.

He waited until they had disappeared before returning to the house, anxious to see where his wayward guest had been secreted.

12

Daytime Nightmare

'In here, boss!'

The urgently melodic summons of Lee Fong saw the rancher and his stalwart bodyguard hustling into the kitchen. They were just in time see Morgan crawling out from under the table which was covered by a large oilcloth upon which the Chinese cook was rolling out some pastry.

'Man, that sure is one helluva hideout,' chuckled the rancher slapping his thighs. 'I'd never have looked under there myself.'

They couldn't resist a hearty laugh. Coated in flour, the fugitive joined in the hilarity. 'It was Fong's idea,' he gasped spitting out a mouthful of white dust. 'I was running round like a headless chicken when Garrety said he was gonna search the place.'

That night they ate a steak pie that tasted all the more appetizing knowing the bizarre circumstances of its preparation.

Early next morning found Morgan preparing to leave. He couldn't allow the Praise B to suffer on account of his problems. It didn't matter that they were not of his making. The facts were clear. He was still a wanted man which meant others would surely come a-searching for him, namely Tubb Ricketts and any other varmints who fancied that reward.

He led the black stallion out of the barn and round to the front of the house before returning to the barn for his bedroll. Suddenly, just like the previous day, a panic-laced holler rent the air as Canute Larsen came galloping back into the corral at full pelt.

'More riders this way coming are,' he panted, urgency making him trip over his rapid-fire dialogue. 'Another lawman as well as Dog boss Top and bunch of cases hard.'

Nobody found the tortured confabulation amusing.

This second bunch had to be the Salida sheriff. And Bishop was certain that T.D. Webb and his gun-slinging minions would have been roped in as deputies. This would be a far more serious encounter than that of the previous day.

'We have to find you a much more secure hidin' place than yesterday. It's a dime to a dozen those critters will insist on rootin' you out if'n I can't persuade them you've split the breeze,' observed Bishop. 'And it won't be no casual pokin' around this time.'

His voice was cracking under the strain, the agile brain racing faster than a desert roadrunner. There was no point berating himself for thinking he could get away with such a reckless attempt to prevent the unjust arrest. All he could do now was issue a silent prayer that he could head them off.

Already, the cloud of dust was rising above the ridge beyond the ranch entrance. Where could he hide the guy?

Then it came to him.

'Over to the main house,' he shouted running across the open ground. 'You boys as well.' This latter directive was aimed at the McCluskey brothers who had been cleaning out the barn.

Bursting through the front door, the rancher made straight for a small room at the rear. He hauled up a trapdoor in the floor revealing a small cellar. It smelt musty and damp having been used for storing potatoes and root crops for use over the winter months.

'Down you go, Morgan,' he pressed. 'It's dark as the grave, but all being well, you won't be in there for long. We'll have to push that heavy dresser over so's the entrance can't be seen.' He quickly helped the fugitive down the steep flight of wooden steps then slammed the door shut.

The last thing Morgan heard was a series of grunts as the oak cabinet was dragged across the floor. All too soon, booted feet clumped across the wooden floor, a door closed, and he was left alone in pitch blackness.

Accompanied by the Swede and Jimbo Dawson, Bishop made for the front of the house appropriating his Bible from a table by the door. Being a man of the cloth, Clay Bishop believed that God would see him through any torment. He had never packed an iron, and had no intention of starting now.

But he offered no objections to his *compadres* toting their own hardware.

The ramrod shot a nervous glance towards the blond Swede regarding the boss's determination to remain unarmed. Canute shrugged his agreement. But both men remained tight-lipped. It was his choice.

Away to the north, dark storm clouds were massing over the Grapes. A roll of thunder echoed across the plains, the mountains were girding up their loins. The rumbling growl was an ominous precursor for the imminent confrontation.

The trio walked purposefully into the middle of the corral, past Canute's vegetable garden, and the horse trough. Then over to the entrance gate. Another two Praise B cowhands joined them, standing to one side, hands nervously resting on the butts of their holstered pistols.

Stopping at the closed gateway with its longhorn adornment, they waited for the arrival of the new posse.

There was no time to feel any sense of fear or trepidation. Within a minute the bunch of riders drew to a halt on the far side of the fence.

Hard faces, mean and devoid of feeling, stared down at the ranch-hands.

The lawman was the first to speak. He repeated the same accusation that Garrety had uttered the previous day adding his own query regarding the outcome of the Green Ridge lawman's quest.

'I'll tell you what I told him,' began the rancher in a brusque outflow meant to signify that the matter was an irritant. 'Two guys came through. I gave them some water and vittles before they left for the border. Don't know who they were, and I don't care. If they've broke the law, that ain't none of my concern.'

'You're lyin', Bishop, you Bible-totin' sonofabitch.' The rancid growl emanated from Thaddeus Webb who nudged his horse through the group to the front. 'And that ain't no idle challenge, mister.'

He leaned over the neck of his horse, a leery smirk etched across the cold contours of his face. A raised arm pointed towards the ranch house.

'All of yuh!' he shouted. 'Cast your eyes over yonder. There's the damn killer's own horse, loaded up and ready to leave. I'd recognize that black with a white splash on its left rump anyplace. And don't you dare deny that Snakeskin Petrie ain't skulkin' in there like the coward he is.'

Bishop didn't need to look round. He cursed himself for making such a stupid error of judgement. They should have left the horse inside the barn.

Webb didn't wait to hear the rancher's reaction. He wanted action, and on his own terms. This jigger was like a boil that needed lancing. And the Top Dog boss was through waiting.

'Now get out of the way 'cos we're comin' through to get that killer and we're gonna hang him from this here gatepost.' Webb leaned down to open the gate. 'And anybody stands in our way'll get a dose of the same.'

'Hold on there, Mister Webb,' interjected Deputy Breckenridge who could see that things were slipping out of control. 'We'll do this in a proper legal manner. Whoever's been breaking the law will be tried and convicted in the proper way. Vigilante law has no place in Freemont County.'

The part-time lawman had been given the job of pursuing the escaped felon by Ricketts who claimed that he had other duties in Salida needing his immediate attention. Breckenridge had not questioned the directive. He had figured this would be his big chance to display the guts and acumen necessary to become a bonafide lawman. Now he wasn't so sure.

Rolling drunks on a Saturday night, or serving notices for unpaid fines was nothing compared to this. Maybe he had taken on more than he could chew.

Still he persisted. 'We have to do this according to the due process,' he muttered. But the order lacked any bite. His next directive was aimed at the unarmed rancher. 'You release this man into my hands, Mister Bishop and we'll say no more about it.'

'Stay where you are!' ordered Bishop taking a step forward. 'Nobody comes through this gate without a proper search warrant. You got one, Deputy?' He was counting on the fact that possession of such a document had never entered the tenderfoot lawman's head.

He was right.

Lined up behind Breckenridge, the other so-called members of the posse were growing restless. Horses were bunching towards the gate. Murmurings of scornful discontent were aimed at the lawman's obsequious tone. This final challenge from the rancher was a step too far. It was the straw that broke the camel's back.

One man broke the threatening stalemate.

'I've had enough of this palaver.' Rufus Cahill had his gun palmed. 'We came here to do a job. So let's get on with it.'

Before anybody knew what was happening his six-gun roared its disapproval. Orange flame and hot lead spat from the jabbering barrel of the Schofield.

Clay Bishop staggered back as three bullets ploughed into him. He went down, and stayed there.

For the briefest of moments, the brutal shock of the cold-blooded attack on an unarmed man stunned the combatants to immobility. Then gunfire erupted from both sides.

Canute managed to get off both barrels of his shotgun before a lethal barrage scythed him down. Before succumbing to the fatal dose of lead poisoning, he did, however, enjoy the satisfaction of witnessing two *desperadoes* throw up their arms as the blast punched them both out of the saddle.

Will Tennant and his buddy Hank Warner drew their pistols and returned fire. Backing away towards the shelter afforded by the horse trough they continued firing until their guns clicked on empty chambers. Only one bullet was on target which struck a horse in the neck, throwing the rider.

These men were cowboys. Their usual gunplay was against varmints and rattlers. Professional gunmen, they most definitely were not.

Neither were they used to reloading at speed.

Will was the first to disappear in a hail of well-placed lead. His partner tried to make a dash for the barn. But he only made it half way before meeting the same fate.

It would be a pronounced understatement to declare that the battle was not going well for the Praise B defenders. Only Jimbo Dawson was left standing, or crouching as he sheltered behind a fence post.

The attackers were now spreading out inside the corral. T.D. Webb made sure that he kept well back from the action. The gang boss was himself no gunman, employing others to do his dirty work.

Breckenridge was in a state of shock. All hell had been unleashed around him. And there was nothing he could do to prevent the blood that was being spilled. Webb noticed the deputy's traumatic state. He was also aware that if this got back to the authorities, awkward questions would be forthcoming.

Sidling up behind the ogling deputy, he drew a small pocket revolver from inside his jacket. Cocking the small gun, he threw a quick glance around to ensure nobody was watching, then pulled the trigger.

The sharp crack was lost amidst the general cacophany. Breckenridge barely exhibited any indication that he had been shot, merely sliding out of the saddle where he lay still.

The battle continued to rage although it was obvious that the attackers were gaining the upper hand. It was equally clear that they had no intention of leaving any witnesses to the slaughter they had instigated.

Over in the barn, Buff McCluskey was livid with rage.

He and his brother only had pistols which were useless at that range. Impotently they looked on as the ranch-hands were cut down one by one. Finally, Buff threw up his arms in despair. He couldn't stand by any longer without retaliating.

Witnessing Thaddeus Webb and his gang taking their revenge on the man who had offered them support following the burning of the store was more than he could stomach.

'I gotta do something,' he yelled. 'These poor guys are being chopped down while we skulk in here like snivelling cowards.' Without another word, Buff charged outside.

'No! No! You'll be killed for sure,' wailed his brother grabbing his arm.

Buff shook him off. Howling like a demented banshee, he scuttled across the open ground of the corral, his revolver spitting poison with every step. Caught by this surprise manoeuvre, one of the assailants clutched at his throat. Another staggered and fell into the horse trough, the dirty water turning a deep shade of crimson.

But it was only a matter of time before the overwhelming firepower of the attackers took the deranged man out.

When his brother finally caught a bullet, Sean rushed out and grabbed the injured man. Desperately, he manhandled him back into the cover of the barn. Somehow, the flying lead missed him.

Quickly he saddled up a couple of horses. He was joined by Jimbo Dawson who had managed to escape detection.

'Come on, Buff,' Sean cried as he heaved his brother up and tried to get him on to a horse. 'We have to get outa here.'

'Leave him be, Sean. He's dead.' The leaden tone of the ramrod passed straight over the Irishman's head.

'No he ain't. I know he ain't. Don't worry, Buff. I'll save yuh.' Tears coarsed down the Irishman's dirt-smeared face as he continued trying to raise the dead weight of the corpse.

'It's no use, Sean.' Jimbo carefully but firmly prised the body away from the stricken man and laid it down on the floor. 'And we'll be joinin' him if'n we don't get outa here pronto.'

He urged the distraught man over to his own horse and levered him into the saddle. Riding out of the door at the rear of the barn, they managed to escape into the labyrinth of hills behind the ranch without being spotted by the attackers.

The gunfire had ceased as the pair spurred away.

The battle of the Praise B was finally over. It had been a daylight nightmare. A bloody scene of carnage and death now stalked the landscape. Those who had survived, professional gunmen all, quickly reloaded their weapons. Grim faces devoid of any sympathy began plundering the dead bodies.

T.D. Webb rode slowly across the open ground and tied his mount beside that of their quarry. Scornful eyes surveyed the bestial looters as they went about their grim task. Cahill joined him.

'Have these scavengers search the whole place.' His voice was flat, imbuing a coldly merciless disregard for the mayhem he had instigated. 'Tear the place apart if'n you have to. But find that killer. We still have a reward to collect.'

Rufus Cahill had every incentive to comply.

But an hour later, he was forced to report the failure of his mission. Webb was seated in the main room. Puffing on a large Havana cigar, a glass of finest French brandy was close at hand. The gang-master's face assumed a sullen cast. This was not what he wanted to hear.

'The bastard has to be around here somewhere.'

'We searched everywhere, TD. And he ain't here.'

A rabid growl issued from Webb's throat. The feral sound was more animal than human. Cahill felt a tremor of fear crawling down his spine.

'We did find one thing though.' Webb

peered across at the hardcase, his brow furrowing. 'Bring him in, boys.'

Lee Fong was frog-marched into the room between two burly toughs.

'So what have we here?' sneered Webb.

'Must be the ranch cook,' said one of the men. 'But we can't get a sensible word out of him.'

A disdainful look of contempt scanned the quaking Chinaman.

'Hang him!' The little guy's eyes bulged. 'He understood that all right,' chortled Webb. 'Tell us where this guy is hidin' and you can go free.'

'Not here, not here,' warbled Lee Fong. 'He escape into hills before sheriff from Green Ridge came yesterday.'

'Think he's telling the truth, boss?' asked Cahill.

'Don't matter none, hang him anyway.'

Lee Fong screamed. Wriggling out of the grip of his captors, he rushed to the door. A single bullet from Cahill's Schofield drilled him in the back.

Webb levered himself out of the comfortable chair and ground the butt end of the cigar under his heel. 'Now burn the whole place to the ground. If the critter's hidin' someplace, that'll flush him out for darned sure.' He moved over to the door. 'Then we'll take what cattle there is around here and rebrand those that ain't been done in Arrowhead Canyon. There's still a lucrative market for beef waitin' for us at Fort Calhoolie.'

13

Praise Be!!

During the battle that was raging above ground, Morgan had fretted and fumed in his subterranean hideaway. Once the shooting started, he had striven with all his might to raise the wooden trapdoor. But without success. The oak dresser was doing its job rather too well. Once again Morgan Silver found himself a prisoner.

All he could do was wait, and trust in the Lord, just like his benefactor was doing. It was a frustrating period made all the more exasperating due to his inability to render assistance. Not to mention the pitch darkness of the cellar. He felt totally helpless, inadequate.

After what seemed a lifetime, in effect little more than ten minutes, the muted rattle of gunfire suddenly ceased. The muscles throughout his whole body tightened. Ears straining to determine what was happening, he remained completely still, hardly daring to breathe. Blood pounded inside his head.

All too soon, the grumble of voices penetrated the thick floorboards overhead. One of them he recognized instantly — Rufus Cahill issuing directions regarding a search of the premises. And Morgan knew exactly who they were hoping to unearth. Surely they couldn't fail to hear the rapid fire beat of his labouring heart.

But the secret hideout had been well chosen.

The angry voices drifted away. He could breathe easily again. Though not for long. His acute sense of smell picked up a strange, rather acrid odour. Twitching nostrils tried to place it.

Smoke!

They had set fire to the ranch house. He would be burnt alive, unable to do a thing to save himself. All too soon, a crackling and snapping of burning timbers could be heard. More smoke filtered down through the floor. The confining dungeon grew hot and airless. Overhead, the disintegrating structure was on the verge of collapse.

But the thick floorboards held firm.

* * *

Morgan had come through the inferno unscathed. Although what good that would do him he had little notion. Unable to escape, he was destined to die of starvation. The single waterbottle would barely get him through another day. Then it would be a painfully lingering death.

Maybe he should end it now before frenzied delirium turned him into a slobbering lunatic. He took out the revolver and cocked it, placing the barrel against his head. His finger tightened on the trigger.

But he did not have the nerve to

follow it through.

With such macabre thoughts juggling for centre stage in his fevered brain, the captive finally succumbed to a fitful sleep.

* * *

The two ranch-hands who had managed to escape unseen reached Fairview later that day. Their meeting with Alice Bishop and her friend was a sombre affair. Relating the outcome of the brutal gun battle and the shooting of her father, not to mention the other hands, was difficult in the extreme.

Night had fallen making it too late to leave for the ranch. And the two escapees were exhausted following the ghastly ordeal.

So here they were approaching the ranch, having pushed the horses at a steady gallop all the way from Fairview. Alice gasped on seeing wisps of smoke rising into the air on the far side of a low knoll.

'The durned skunks have fired the ranch!' exclaimed Sean McCluskey.

Spurring forward, urged on by a frantic dread of what she would discover, Alice led the way.

The sight that met her bulging eyes was all she had been dreading, and more. Blackened beams of the once proud ranch poked from among the torched ruins. It was heart-rending to see. Only the barn had been spared. Unable to maintain her stoic bearing any longer, Alice burst into tears when she spotted her father's body lying amidst the bloody carnage.

The others remained silent, shifting uncomfortably in their saddles. Humble cowpokes, they were at a loss where comforting the opposite sex was concerned.

It was Cock-eyed Sam who finally took the lead. Nudging his mount down the slope, the others followed slowly, hardly daring to look upon the appalling scene of devastation. Bodies lay strewn about. Some they recognized. Over by the horse trough were Will Tennant and his buddy, Hank Warner. And the big Swede, Canute Larsen whose prized garden had been trampled into mush.

But of Morgan Silver there was no sign. The pair had said their goodbyes before she left for Fairview. It had been a tearful parting although Morgan promised to return once his name had been cleared. So at least she knew that he must have got away unscathed.

Nobody could place the other bodies scattered about. The implication was that at least the defenders had put up a good account of themselves before they were overwhelmed.

Scavenging buzzards rose into the air cawing angrily at having been denied a rampant feast.

Meanwhile, Alice had rushed over to her father's shattered body. Sinking down on to her knees, the girl couldn't bring herself to look into his lifeless eyes. Then a miracle occurred. For a brief moment, Alice stared at the recumbent form unable to comprehend what she had just witnessed.

A strident call punctuated the heavily morbid atmosphere. The stunned cowboys swung towards the girl's impassioned outcry.

'He's alive! Pa's still breathing!'

Gently she raised the dust-smeared head. Whispering endearments, she dribbled some much needed water between the bleeding lips. Clutched in his hand was the Word of God. Smashed and holed in three places, Clay Bishop's faith in his Maker had been answered. The heavy Bible had saved his life.

Two bullets were stuck fast inside the holy tome. A third had gone right through but had been deflected into his chest. It had missed his heart by a whisker and passed right through the rib cage and out the far side. The wound was serious, but not life threatening.

'Help me get him into the barn.'

Sam effortlessly lifted the rancher into his sturdy arms. Together the revitalized group hustled across the yard. Carefully they laid him down on the straw in one of the empty stalls.

'We'll go see about layin' out the poor jaspers that didn't make it,' intoned the dolorous voice of Jimbo Dawson. He nodded to Sean McCluskey and the pair moved away. Sam nodded his approval of the suggestion.

Meanwhile, Morgan Silver had stumbled out from the griping torpor of a phlegmatic sleep. Inside the stygian confines of his dungeon, nothing had changed. Or had it? Something had jolted him back to ill-favoured wakefulness. He strained to hear, listening for some vital clue that he was no longer alone.

A discordant yell penetrated his addled brain. And it was no ordinary cry for help. He recognized it instantly as that of Alice Bishop. In no time he was clambering up the wooden steps and hammering on the trap door with the butt of his pistol. When he tried hollering to be let out, a hoarse rasp was all that emerged. The dust and smoke had dried up his throat, effectively choking off his vocal chords.

Jimbo and his partner had just begun the gruesome business of moving the blooded corpses when they both heard the knocking.

'Hear that, Jimbo?' queried McCluskey pausing in his task.

'Sure did,' concurred the ramrod. 'And its comin' from the main house. Somebody's trapped in there.'

'It must be that guy who the boss helped to escape.'

'Gee!' blurted Jimbo. 'I'd plumb forgotten all about that jigger.'

They hurried over to the shattered ruins and began to carefully pick a way through the still smouldering debris. It was a delicate task as the charred timbers were threatening to crumble at any moment. The constant rapping appeared to be emanating from the rear of the wreckage proving that their supposition had been correct.

'OK!' shouted Jimbo to let the

trapped man know he had been heard. 'We're comin'.'

Scrambling through the chaotic devastation, they reached the back room.

'He's still down there under the floor,' observed Sean McCluskey. 'Help me get this dresser out the way.'

'Thank the Lord you came.' The weak croak of exultation filtered up from the depths. 'Reckoned I was a goner.'

Soon they had the stricken prisoner released from his tomb. Morgan screwed up his eyes against the harsh light of day. It took some moments for his pounding heart to settle before he was able to convey his thanks to the rescuers. The sight that unfolded as he peered around was like a badly painted tableau from the underworld.

Gingerly the two rescuers led the unsteady man out of the wrecked house where the full picture of the tragedy was revealed in all its hideous reality.

Morgan was lost for words. All he could do was stare open-mouthed at the wholesale butchery that had been perpetrated. Thaddeus Webb and the rest of those scumbags from the Top Dog had much to answer for.

'Any other survivors'?' The question emerged as a stifled croak.

'Only Mister Bishop,' replied Jimbo. 'Seems like his belief in the Good Book paid off.' Morgan shot him a quizzical frown. 'Miss Alice is seeing to him over in the barn.'

After checking the old rancher would not be keeping his appointment with the scythe man, Morgan's reunion with Alice was anything but restrained. Throwing herself into his arms she desperately clung to the lean torso. They kissed ardently, oblivious to the grinning faces around them. Even Sean McCluskey allowed himself a tight smile before laying his brother's corpse down with the others ready for burial.

Alice's questions regarding Morgan's unexpected appearance poured forth in a torrent of exhuberant bursts. It all ended in more tears when he informed her that he was going after the perpetrators of the heinous onslaught. And he was going alone.

'You need to get your father to the doctor in Fairview,' he insisted stroking her red tresses to restore calm and common sense following a heated persistence that she would accompany him. 'If'n he don't get proper medical treatment soon, he'll not make it.' His next comment was to Cock-eyed Sam. 'You go with her and take the wagon.' The negro gently held the girl's arms as Morgan mounted the black. 'And I'll meet you both in Fairview when this business is settled.'

'At least take someone with you,' Alice persisted. 'Those critters play for keeps. And one man alone don't stand a chance.'

'I'll ride with you, Mister Silver.' The offer came from Sean McCluskey who hurried to justify his proposal. 'Sure as eggs is eggs it was T.D. Webb who had my store burned down. Nothing would give me greater pleasure than to see that lowlife skunk get his just desserts.'

'Sounds good to me,' agreed Morgan. 'And Jimbo here can track down the place where the varmints have hidden those rustled cattle with the Box 8 brand. My guess is they'll hunker down some place to give the mavericks the same brand before pushing on to Fort Calhoolie.'

'Where are you headin' then?' asked the ramrod.

'I've got me a date with one of the Top Dog minions who stole my grubstake.' The reply emerged as a low growl. 'By leaving now, we could catch him red-handed afore he has time to join the rest of the gang.'

14

The Worm Turns

Thaddeus Webb was stamping around his office like a bear with a sore head. He drew heavily on a big cigar, pumping out clouds of blue smoke. Things had definitely not gone according to plan. Not only had they failed to locate the escaped killer, Snakeskin Bob Petrie, but half his men were out of action. Two had been killed and three others were badly wounded and being treated by the horse doctor.

The only good to come out of this was liquidating Bishop and appropriating some of his cattle. Although the other small operators in the county would doubtless rally to his daughter's side once they discovered what had happened.

The situation in Salida was becoming too overheated.

The Top Dog boss knew that the writing was on the wall. He had underestimated the influence that Bishop had over the smaller outfits. To add insult to injury, his spies had brought the news that his probity was under question. Some were even threatening to remove their savings from the unofficial bank.

And then there was that Green Ridge sheriff. The jasper would be back if'n he failed to catch up with Petrie. And he'd want answers that Webb was loath to supply.

The hustler paused in mid-stride having reached a decision.

There was enough hard cash in the safe to set him up in business some place else. His eyes misted over. He had always harboured a notion to settle down in California. Now was his chance.

Without further ado, he moved across to the safe. Deftly manipulating the combination lock, he swung open the heavy steel door. Stacks of used notes lay piled up in thousand dollar bands.

There must have been at least thirty grand staring at him. Yes indeed, muttered the devious miscreant to himself. There was more than enough here to provide Thaddeus D. Webb with a life of luxury for the rest of his days.

The fact that a substantial quantity of the money was being held for depositors who wanted a safe haven for their cash completely failed to dent the swindler's conscience.

T.D. Webb felt no hint of remorse for his despicable actions. The money was there, and it was his for the taking.

Quickly he began to stuff his saddle-bags with the loot.

His horse was round the back of the store. Those of his men who had been left unscathed were avidly toasting the memory of their deceased sidekicks down in the bar. So here was a heaven-sent opportunity to sneak away from Salida and disappear.

Opening the office door, he peered out into the corridor. It was empty.

A few steps brought him to the rear door at the back. It opened on to a flight of steps that led down to a stable yard.

From there it would be a short ride through the amalgam of back lots, tents and shacks to reach the foothills where he could quickly lose himself amidst the maze of draws and arroyos. It was a propitious omen that darkness was fast draping its umbrid tentacles across the wild landscape.

Webb allowed himself a half smile as he pulled open the door.

'Goin' somewhere, TD?'

The swindler's escape was halted in its tracks. Stunned by this sudden jolt to his plans, Webb's lower jaw flopped open. Both eyes popped.

'And it looks like you're aimin' to take a vacation.' The mocking tones of Rufus Cahill drilled into the gang leader's sluggish brain. Hard, flinty orbs focused on the bulging saddle-bags. 'Now that ain't very sociable, Thaddeus. Goin' off like that without tellin' your buddies.'

Webb was crowded back into the corridor by the burly outlaw.

'I-I didn't expect you back here until tomorrow,' he stuttered dragging a hand across the runnels of sweat beading his forehead. 'You f-finished branding them m-mavericks early, then?'

'I left Dallas Biglow and two more of the boys doin' that,' he hissed in a flat voice devoid of emotion. 'As for me, I had this tickling round the back of my ear. Just couldn't get rid of it.' With meaningful intent, Cahill rubbed at the offending appendage. His hooded gaze gripped the nervous Webb, mesmeric and unyielding just like a stalking fox. 'Ump! There it is again. Yuh know what that means?'

Webb just stared at him as he was slowly forced back into the office. A mirthless cackle spat from between the outlaw's warped lips. He pushed the cheating rogue hard in the chest sending him staggering against the still-open door of the safe.

'Means that some'n wasn't right. Some cheatin' skunk was after runnin' out on his buddies.' Cahill grabbed the fancy ruffled shirt of the quaking braggart. Buttons popped as the material ripped. 'Seems that my old hunchbender was right again, don't it, mister?' The grip tightened as Cahill unfastened one of the bags with his other hand. 'And that goldarned empty safe proves it.'

'No, no. you got it all wrong, Rufus,' wheedled the blustering scapegrace. 'I-I was coming to join you and the boys at Arrowhead Canyon. Then we could split the dough before driving the cattle to Fort Calhoolie.'

Webb's pleading eyes urged the other man to believe his denial of any underhanded chicanery. It was a convincing ploy. If nothing else, T.D. Webb knew he had the cunning wit to get his own way in any situation. Why else had he become Top Dog? 'I ain't the sort of guy who would cheat on his confederates. It just ain't my style.'

Cahill's blunt-edged vow to kill the swindler was wavering. Could he be telling the truth?

Webb saw the indecision in the lowered gaze. His right hand slid down and into the pocket of his jacket. Gripping the butt of a small up-and-over derringer, he suddenly pushed the outlaw away and drew the tiny pistol. Two bullets erupted from the short barrel.

But Rufus Cahill was faster. He had not escaped justice for this long without reading an opponent's body language.

Seeing the avaricious glint in Webb's eyes, he threw himself to one side. Palming his own revolver he pumped four shots into the devious rat. Webb tottered, bewildered by the sudden change in fortune. Keeling over he slid out of sight behind a heavy oak desk.

The derringer might have been one

of the smallest firearms on the frontier, but its .41 load packed a hefty wallop. Both slugs had struck home.

Unfortunately, Tubb Ricketts had chosen that moment to collect his monthly bonus. It was a fateful decision from which there was no comeback. Clutching his chest, the sheriff reeled, then slid down the wall of the corridor where he sat opened mouthed. Dead as a Boot Hill epitaph.

Cahill grabbed a bottle of Scotch and gulped down a hefty measure. The hard liquor burnt his throat, but settled his jangling nerve ends.

His face cracked into a malevolent grin. He could imagine how folks would see it. Ricketts had finally decided that the Top Dog proprietor had gone too far and needed to have his wings clipped. A difference of opinion had led to the gunfight in which both protagonists had shot each other.

Bad luck for Ricketts, but a welcome result for Rufus Cahill.

So he had been right after all. Webb

had been intending to run out on them with all the dough he had amassed. And now it all belonged to Rufus Cahill. All he had to do was dig up the two grand secreted at the shack before driving the stolen cattle to market. Cahill punched the air in delight. Then it would be:

Montana! Here I come!

There was no time to lose. Quickly, the outlaw stuck his own pistol into the hand of the sheriff while purloining the lawdog's Colt Peacemaker for his own use. The same ruse had worked like a dream up in Green Ridge. There was no reason why it should not afford the same result in Salida when Garrety returned, which he surely would at some point.

Once accomplished, the outlaw slipped away with his booty before any curious drinkers from the bar downstairs came a-snooping.

15

Starbreaker

Following the trail left by the rustlers proved to be easy. They had made no attempt on this occasion to conceal the theft. Sean McCluskey was eager to catch up with Thaddeus Webb to exact full retribution for his brother's death and the burning down of their store. He kept pushing ahead. Even when Morgan urged caution in order to conserve their mounts, the Irishman ignored the advice, such was the intensity of his wrath.

When they reached the low hillock overlooking the old camp of the rustlers, Morgan insisted that his partner curb his provocation.

'Going off half cocked like a loose cannon,' he persisted with vigour, 'could get us both killed without completing what we set out for. You don't want that, do you?'

'Guess you're right, Morg,' replied his contrite sidekick. 'But it makes me see red just thinkin' on what that scumbag did to me and Buff.'

'Don't worry none,' advocated Morgan gripping his shoulder. 'These skunks are going to eat dirt afore the day's out.'

He was about to move down the slope when a plume of dust caught his eye. Someone was approaching, and at speed. Both men ducked low, waiting to ascertain who this mysterious rider could be. A mutual intimation concluded that it had to be one or more of the gang.

The rider came ripping over the plains at a fast lick. Skidding to halt outside the old lean-to, he leapt from the saddle and hustled inside. It was impossible to identify the newcomer due to the billowing cloud of yellow dust.

Morgan took the opportunity to creep down the slope while the guy was otherwise occupied inside the shack. They took up positions on either side of the entrance behind stands of juniper and cholla cactus.

Twenty minutes passed before the stranger emerged. He was carrying a saddle-bag over his left shoulder. In his right was a shovel which he now threw aside.

Morgan tensed. Every nerve in his body was tingling. He would recognize that beard and the red vest anywhere. And the guy was toting his very own bag, doubtless containing the two grand he'd stolen. Cahill must have buried the loot in the shack and had now returned to retrieve it. That implied he was intending to quit the territory.

Morgan unhooked the hammer thong and loosened the revolver in its holster as he stepped out from cover. Cahill had his back to the fuming victim of his vile actions.

Morgan coughed. A deliberate sound to attract the varmint's attention.

Cahill's back stiffened.

'Stand up and turn around,' spat the wronged man. 'And make it nice and slow. I wouldn't want to kill a man without him knowing the reason.'

'Well, well,' chuckled the outlaw, unphased by the sudden change of circumstances. 'So we meet again. You just won't lie down, will yuh fella? I should have let Selman gun you down when I had the chance.'

'Keep your mitts in the air,' ordered Morgan brusquely. He was not about to be hoodwinked by any tricky manoeuvres from the killer.

The outlaw slowly complied.

That was when Morgan's legs turned to jelly. He felt the blood rush to his head. His gun hand wavered. A fearful trembling wracked his whole body while staring at the critter's forearm.

Cahill had rolled up the sleeves of his shirt while digging for the hidden loot. And there it was, gleaming in the morning sunlight. A purple birthmark in the shape of a five-pointed star.

But the outlaw was totally unware

that Snakeskin Bob Petrie and this critter were one and the same. Sensing his opponent's unexpected loss of concentration, Cahill's hand dropped towards his holstered revolver.

'Hold it. mister,' barked another voice from the far side of the clearing. 'You heard the man. And if'n he don't kill yuh, I surely will.' Sean McCluskey's Navy Colt gestured with menacing intent.

His partner's timely intervention jerked Morgan back to the reality of his situation. Shaking off the painful recollection which had dulled his mind and wrenched at his guts, he offered his partner a grateful nod of thanks. If Sean hadn't stepped in, he might well have thrown away any chance he had been given to confront the rat who had turned him into a wanted criminal.

He took a step forward, his gun hand steady as a rock.

Blazing eyes concentrated on the bizarre mark. There was no doubting that it was the one he had seen in the assay agent's office in Green Ridge. So

Rufus Cahill was indeed the real killer. And here he was. Arms raised and at the mercy of his one-time victim.

'Know who I am, Rufus?' The query was delivered in a deadpan lifeless inflection.

Cahill shrugged. This was the guy he had robbed of two grand and left tied to a tree on the Chavez Saltflats. That was his sole recollection.

Morgan appeared to read his thoughts.

'No! Not that robbery. The one in' — a macabre gleam lit up his face as he paused deliberately for effect — 'Green Ridge. Remember the assay office, and the poor sucker who took your rap?'

Bulging eyes were enough to convey the fact that the blunt message had struck home with a vengeance.

'You!' The blood drained from the killer's face. His black beard quivered as the truth rapidly suffused his whole being.

'It was the birthmark,' said Morgan. 'Like having a notice pinned to your head.' He paused, grinning at the shocked outlaw before continuing. 'I could just gun you down right here in cold blood, and nobody would blame me.'

Sean McCluskey voiced his agreement as his sidekick went on in the same even tone. 'But I ain't that sort of guy. Not like some.' The latter remark was delivered with a touch of acerbic bitterness. Slowly he replaced the revolver in its holster.

'So I'm gonna give you an even break. And Sean here will be the referee.'

His narrowed gaze never left the outlaw. Cahill responded with a disdainful leer. He had been given a lifeline and intended to make full use of it, convinced that he could outdraw this jackass in any one-to-one gunfight.

'You give the word and we go for it,' Morgan pressed the bemused Irishman. 'And if'n things don't go my way, he goes free. Agreed?'

McCluskey could only nod his head absently.

'And just to ensure the rat don't pull any fancy tricks, we empty our guns apart from keeping one shell apiece up the spout.' Morgan moved across to the hovering outlaw. 'Keep him well covered, Sean, while I empty both our guns.'

With infinite caution, he levered out the shells leaving a single round in both barrels. Then he slipped Cahill's pistol back into its holster. Stepping back, both men stood facing each other, hands hovering like claws above their holstered guns.

'Ready when you are, Sean.' The order to commence the final showdown emerged as little more than a harsh whisper.

The Irishman coughed nervously, then drew hard on his pipe.

'I'll set my time piece to alarm mode,' he said. 'When the music ends, a bell will ring. And that'll be your cue to — ' He breathed deeply, looking at both protagonists in turn.

Nods of understanding followed from

both parties as the tinny sound of 'Oh Susannah!' began echoing across the killing ground. The spritely tune was totally out of keeping with the sombre proceedings being enacted. A surreal nightmarish scenario presided over by a pipe-smoking Irishman.

Without any warning the music stopped, a brief pause and the alarm bell rang out.

Both men grabbed for their weapons. Cahill was a half second faster on the draw but his aim was awry. His shot tore a lump from Morgan's right ear. It was painful but not serious. Morgan yelled out clutching at the bleeding lobe. Recovering quickly, he aimed his pistol.

A blanching finger tightened on the trigger. Then he hesitated. How could he shoot down an unarmed man?

Cahill immediately sensed his opponent's vacillation. But the outlaw harboured no such scruples. He uttered a rabid guffaw, his left hand reached into the pocket of his red vest. It emerged clutching the derringer appropriated from the deceased Thaddeus Webb.

Two shots split the ether.

Both took the devious killer in the chest. A wave of shocked realization washed over the outlaw's ashen features. In the excitement of the dramatic showdown, he had completely forgotten about the referee and his part in the proceedings.

'Some guys just don't play by the rules,' chided the Irishman standing up. Blowing smoke from the pistol barrel, he turned to address the injured opponent who had clamped his necker to the bleeding appendage. 'And you shouldn't be so darned high moralled about rubbin' out a skunk.'

'I ain't never shot a man in cold blood, and I ain't about to start now,' countered Morgan firmly. Continuing in a more grateful vein, he added, 'but I sure am obliged for your intervention.'

Both men laughed as the tension drained from their bodies.

Morgan walked across to the dying man and bent down. Quickly he kicked the small derringer out of reach of a searching hand.

'Where's Webb then?' he inquired tersely.

The dying man coughed, hawking up a spout of bright red. 'He . . . didn't . . . make it.' A few rasping breaths were squeezed out of the punctured lungs before the final deathly comment, 'and neither . . . did I.'

Even though Morgan Silver, just like Snakeskin Bob Petrie, was no cold-hearted killer, he could dredge up little sympathy for the dead outlaw. Good riddance, as far as he was concerned.

He moved across to where Cahill had dropped the saddle-bag. All the money was still inside, untouched. Meanwhile, Sean McCluskey was examining the outlaw's own saddle pack. He gave a sharp whistle of surprise on discovering the contents.

'Take a look at this,' he exclaimed. 'I ain't never seen this kinda dough before. There must be thousands stuffed in here.'

'Looks like Cahill and his boss had a disagreement over sharing out the loot,' Morgan observed thoughtfully. 'After the depositors have been repaid, there should be enough left over to rebuild your store in Salida and the Praise B ranch house.

'First off though, we have to find those rustlers.' Now that the initial euphoria of having retrieved his stolen money was dissipating, Morgan's attention returned to this unfinished matter. 'Although I don't figure those guys will put up much of a fight when they hear that both their bosses have quit the scene.'

'We can call on Butch Jarman of the Lazy J ranch to help us out,' interjected McCluskey. 'His ranch is only a half day's ride from here. And I know for a fact he had strong suspicions about Webb and his dealings. That's why he stayed with me when the bastard began issuing his threats.'

Both men spun round as the pounding of hoofs assailed their ears. Guns drawn and ready, they ducked behind a nearby clump of mesquite. A single rider emerged from the haze. Before the charging mustang had juddered to a halt the guy had leapt from the saddle. The manoeuvre displayed all the deft fluidity of a skilled cowhand.

The waiting duo relaxed as Jimbo Dawson hurried across.

'I followed their trail,' he panted through rapid gasps of breath. 'And it led to a closed-off draw known as Arrowhead Canyon. I climb up the rocks near the entrance to get me a good look.' He paused to draw breath. 'Any of you guy's gotten a smoke?'

Morgan tossed him the makings. Rolling a quirley, the Praise B ramrod suddenly noticed the body of Rufus Cahill.

'Looks as if you fellas have been busy.' The comment was casually delivered. Then his nonchalent pose stiffened as recognition of the dead outlaw materialized. 'That's the low-down skunk that shot down the boss.'

He walked across and gave the splayed out torso a brutal kick.

'About those rustlers,' Morgan said bringing the conflab back to the matter in hand. 'How many are in the gang?'

'I counted four,' replied Jimbo puffing hard on the thin quirley. 'They looked to be almost finished with the brandin' when I left.'

'They'll be waiting on this critter to turn up before driving them to Fort Calhoolie,' observed Morgan thoughtfully.

'I was tellin' Morg here that we could get help from Butch Jarman at the Lazy J,' Sean McCluskey added.

'Good idea,' agreed Jimbo. 'Butch had no time for Webb and his bunch.'

'One of you guys help me get this corpse into the shack,' said Morgan. On seeing their puzzled frowns, he explained that Cahill was the killer who had framed him. 'The body is needed to clear my name when I catch up with the Green Ridge sheriff.' He moved across to mount the black stallion. 'It's a long story, boys. I'll tell you on the way to the Lazy J.'

* * *

Butch Jarman had been more than willing to help apprehend the rustlers. The grizzled old rancher had also been the victim of cattle thefts in recent weeks. Along with Morgan and his buddies, five other cowhands had surreptitiously enclosed the rustling gang in a pincer movement. There was no escape from the Arrowhead.

Once his men were in place, Morgan hollered down to the outlaws who were sitting round a campfire, ostensibly awaiting their boss.

'It's all over, boys!' The blunt declaration boomed across the rock-enclosed basin. 'Webb and Cahill are both dead and we have you surrounded. So the healthy option is to throw down your weapons and surrender.'

The three rustlers leapt to their feet. Staring around, fear was written on their hard-bitten features. Dallas Biglow went for his gun and started blasting aimlessly at the invisible antagonists. It was a futile action that resulted in a lethal retaliation from the hidden cowboys. Like a dancing marionette the gunman flopped around as hot lead peppered his body.

The deadly exchange lasted no more than ten seconds. Then silence once again descened over the hidden enclave.

'What's it to be?' called Morgan standing up and showing himself. 'You boys want to go the way of your buddies?'

Two pairs of hands grasped at the hot air.

'Don't shoot, we surrender!' shouted Mace Honniker.

Slowly, the concealed cowboys emerged from cover. Maintaining a watchful eye on their adversaries, they zig-zagged down through the clumps of sagebrush and prickly pear that cloaked the lower slopes of Arrowhead Canyon.

The doleful pair of rustlers were quickly disarmed and tethered to their horses. Meanwhile, Butch Jarman had been examining the re-branded cattle.

He gave a whistle that hinted of relief mixed with admiration. 'Ain't no denyin' that these varmints were experts with a runnin' iron. These brands are works of art. Only a real cattle man could ever have told the difference. Another week and the burnt hide would have healed to blend perfectly into a fresh brand. The Cattlemen's Association will need to verify their cancellation before any legitimate sale can be made.'

Soon the small herd was back on the trail. The drive split up after an hour. Jarman pushed all the cattle back to his spread. He would keep them there until such time as the Praise B was back in business.

Morgan and the Praise B riders then

headed for Fairview with their two prisoners after picking up the body of Rufus Cahill. Seeing the blooded corpse of the deceased outlaw effectively staunched any thought the rustlers might have harboured regarding an escape attempt.

A half hour passed with no comments being offered on their recent experiences. Only the welcome trilling of larks and the gentle plod of hoofs intruded on the tranquil calm.

It was Jimbo Dawson who broke the easy silence.

'You figure maybe in the not too distant future, I might be havin' to don my best suit?' A wry smirk creased the ramod's furrowed contours. It was matched by the equally wide grin of Sean McCluskey.

Morgan frowned. 'What you boys driving at?'

'The old timer is trying to hint that there might possibly be a wedding due soon,' spelled out the breezy Irishman.

'Who's getting married?' replied

Morgan deliberately playing the simpleton.

There followed a gently mocking shake of the head from Jimbo.

'This fella needs leading by the hand.'

THE END